THE SCHOOL PRINCIPAL

Studies in Middle Eastern Literatures – Number Four

JALAL AL-e AHMAD

The School Principal
A NOVEL

Translated from the Persian by John K. Newton
Introduction and Notes by Michael C. Hillmann

BIBLIOTHECA ISLAMICA
Minneapolis

Copyright © 1974 by Bibliotheca Islamica, Inc.
Manufactured in the United States of America
Library of Congress Catalog Card Number: 74-80599
ISBN: 0-88297-032-1

BIBLIOTHECA ISLAMICA, INC./Booksellers and Publishers
Box 14474 University Station
Minneapolis, Minnesota 55414/U.S.A.

CONTENTS

Introduction ☐ page 7
Notes ☐ page 29
The School Principal ☐ page 35
Glossary ☐ page 136

INTRODUCTION

Jalāl Āl-e Aḥmad's first book, *The Exchange of Visits* (1946), is a collection of twelve stories that presage what were to be Āl-e Aḥmad's basic and permanent concerns in writing: the critical exposition of problems in contemporary Iranian society and the identification of forces, internal and external, that play a part in the way many Iranians think, feel, and behave. In these first stories, Āl-e Aḥmad likewise reveals several basic and enduring characteristics of his writing craft: an eye for detail, an ear for the rhythms and idiom of colloquial speech, and a feel for the drama that the commonplace and apparently undramatic afford a narrative artist.

The following translation of a representative, if very brief, story from *The Exchange of Visits*, serves to illustrate Āl-e Aḥmad's early short fiction:

"The China Flowerpot"[1]

The bus filled up and started to move. The last person to board was carrying a valuable, antique, china flowerpot and, trying to maintain his balance, headed warily toward the rear of the bus. There, the people in the back seat jostled each other and somehow found room for the man with the china flowerpot. He was a man of forty or more, wearing a stylish overcoat and a smart, new hat. The hand that gripped the flowerpot was incased in a new leather glove.

There were four other passengers in the back seat: two women in full-length *chādor** veils who were laughing almost hysterically at some private matter, and two other persons, one an old man, bent and preoccupied, and the other a devil-may-care sort wearing neither shirt collar nor necktie. His shirt sleeves, their cuff buttons long since come off, protruded beyond the cuffs of his stiff, starchy trenchcoat. His hair fell below and outside a beat-up hat. A grey, mottled beard covered his freckled face, right up to beneath his eyes.

From the moment the dapper one, flowerpot in hand, sat down next to this latter, he attracted the whole

---

*Persian words and phrases and other items relating to Iran italicized in the text are defined or explained in the glossary at the end of this volume.

attention and thoughts of the latter, whose eyes riveted upon the flowerpot.

The owner of the flowerpot sat quietly. He set the flowerpot on his knee and held it by its base. With his ungloved hand, he jingled some small coins. But his neighbor, totally absorbed in scrutinizing the flowerpot, appeared agitated. He raised and lowered his head, tilted it this way and that, striving, however possible, to observe this delicate and beautiful flowerpot more closely. Perhaps for the first time in his life he was face to face with beauty; or if not, perhaps it was the first time he comprehended the meaning of beauty.

It was a fine china vase. On its two slender handles a design had been so artfully painted that the handles seemed to merge into the painted background of the body of the vase and could be distinquished only with difficulty. It was so fine and delicate that it transmitted the light coming through the bus window and gleaming on it, and cast a pulsating shadow on the leather glove of its owner's hand.

The fellow in the raincoat had by now viewed all the details of the side of the vase facing him; but he was not content with that. At every corner the bus negotiated, the passengers then lurching to the opposite side, he took advantage of the moment and slouched a bit more in the direction of the vase owner so that he might get a glimpse at that side of the vase as well. He tried hard, but without much success. Finally, after priming himself a couple times and throwing out his chest, he spoke--the vase owner by now aware of his neighbor's discomfiture--:

"Excuse me, sir. Would it be possible for me to take a look at your flowerpot?"

"Certainly, by all means. My pleasure. It's really nothing much."

And presenting the vase two-handedly and somewhat cautiously to his dishevelled neighbor, he added: "But I beg you..." The other cut him off abruptly and said: "Please rest assured. With the utmost caution. I won't be that long."

) 9 (

And he began inspecting the vase. From the front and the back. From beneath and above. He even scrutinized the vase's interior. In the meantime, the owner's eyes followed the latter's hands. And although the former tried to present an image of unconcern, while he kept his head facing forward and endeavored to read the brass, prayer-formula medallion tacked on the roof above the bus driver's head, from the corner of his eye he surveyed the vase and the movements of the hand of his neighbor, who, having inspected the whole vase, now held it up to the bus window. He put his hand in front of the vase and examined the pale red light that was reflected through the vase and around his fingers and the shadow of his own hand that slightly darkened the interior of the vase. By moving the vase forward and backward in relation to the bus window, he increased and diminished the colorful and detailed chiaroscuro effect...

...At another corner, the bus turned. And the passengers, caught unawares, jostled one another. He likewise lurched, tottered, and having no rail or grip by which to maintain his balance, unwittingly released his hand from the base of the vase and let it go...and the vase fell and, with a barely audible noise, broke into three pieces.

The bus hadn't yet fully negotiated the turn when the groan of the vase owner rose up: "Oh, no!" And he said nothing else, but merely stared in bewilderment at the pieces of the vase. His nonchalant neighbor bent over, and, while retrieving the vase pieces, said: "It's all right. Nothing really happened." Thereupon, the vase owner, who had just returned to his senses, suddenly burst like a pomegranate and, colored with adrenalin, roared: "What else could happen that wouldn't be all right?"

"Nothing, Āqā. Listen. The vase just broke. That's all. It was just one of those things."

"What!? You bum. You've got some nerve."

"Āqā, maintain your dignity, please. Why say things that don't make sense?"

"You say it's nonsense. You son of a bitch. If you hadn't seen the vase, would your cross-eyes have gone blind?"

At this point, the others realized what had happened. One of the women seated next to the men assumed a compassionate mien and said: "Oh, dear. What a beautiful vase it was. What a pity. But, *Aqā* is right. *C'est la vie.*" The owner of the vase cut her off thusly: "Madam, what are you saying? I paid seventy-five *tomans* for that vase. You think that's nothing?" The culprit added: "Okay. Granted. What's to be done about it? Give it to someone to put together again..." The other woman spoke up from beneath her prayer shawl: "Fine, brother. But what happened? Are you all thumbs?" To which the culprit, while arguing with the vase owner and without turning his head toward the woman, replied: "Lady, no one told you to stick your nose in."

"Well, I never...God bless us. The owner's right, absolutely right. This guy has some nerve. He wants to bite my head off."

The vase owner had just bent over. Having removed his glove, while holding the vase pieces in his hand, he shouted: "I thought I was being neighborly. We're a nation worth nothing. And now that the vase is broken, he says it was fate. He thinks I'm going to let him go. Well, I'm going to collect the last penny of the price of the vase. You'd think money was hay. I buy a vase. You break it. Then you say, 'Have it fixed.' You spastic. What's an antique to you? You haven't even the brains to look at one. Of course, I'm a fool for treating a lummox like him with kindness."

And, as the bus reached a station, he added: "*Aqā*. Stop the bus. The police station's near here. Let me exercise my duty toward this man..." And, standing up, he turned toward the driver and said, "*Aqā*, don't let him get off till I bring a policeman and have all the passengers attest to what happened..."

And before he reached the door, he turned, standing

) 11 (

in the center of the bus, and repeated his request to all the passengers and proceeded to get off, once more persuading the driver not to drive away.

Some of the passengers discussed the incident among themselves. A couple people merely watched and laughed. The two women were still giggling, but no one paid them any attention. The culprit talked to himself: "Okay. What can be done? It's not that I did it on purpose. So it fell and broke..."

The driver's assistant was crying out, hawking for customers.

The vase owner had gone some twenty paces from the bus. The bus driver, who had spent a couple minutes motionless and sunk in thought, stirred, straightened himself behind the wheel, called to his assistant, put his foot on the accelerator and took off...

The passengers were dumbstruck, their mouths hung open. And the driver's assistant, in answer to these mute protests, spoke up from his stool: "Okay. What business was it of ours? Someone else has broken a vase. Are we supposed to stay put and do nothing?"

The vase owner was hurrying toward the police station. He suddenly sensed what was happening. He turned and raised his hands as if to prevent the bus from leaving. But the bus merely swerved a bit and went on. He cried out: "Stop...stop them...vase... the poor driver...hey, officer."

Seeing his state, the passengers began to laugh. Policemen now surrounded the vase owner and were inquiring what happened. But he merely cried out: "Stop them...seventy-five *tomans*...the lummox...a china flowerpot...they've gone...what was the license number...officer!"

In a sense, "The China Flowerpot" and other stories in *The Exchange of Visits* reveal Āl-e Aḥmad at an extreme in his career as a writer, that of the narrative artist for whom social issues and problems lurk partly delineated or merely hinted at amid the single incident or tissue of events that is his focus. At the other extreme, making use of the same flair for directness, economy, and forceful flow and flexibility of prose, Āl-e Aḥmad becomes the angry and ironic essayist and social commentator of *Weststruckness* (1962), his most influential piece of nonfiction, a lengthy essay describing the nature and citing the ill effects of Iran's confrontation with, and ultimate submission to, the West during the past three centuries, especially during this century.

Illustrative of Āl-e Aḥmad as essayist and social critic is the following translation of chapter 9 of *Weststruckness:*

"What are Education and the University Accomplishing?"[2]

"Let's now take a look at society from the viewpoint of education. It's a window from within whose four sides my gaze has always focussed. In terms of education, we strongly resemble wild grass. There's a piece of ground; and a seed from somewhere, brought by the wind or in a bird's beak, falls onto it; and the rain likewise helps the grass to grow. In like fashion, we construct a school anyway we know how— in order to increase the property value of the surrounding area—or to realize the pretensions of some landowner with clout—or in the name of redressing grievances which such-and-such a tyrant wrought through pillage— or through the sincere efforts of the inhabitants of a village—or by means of the endowment of a third of the wealth of some deceased individual—in whatever form and through whatever means, once the school's built, the apparatus and appurtenances of education also suddenly spring into existence there; and however it happens, one of the fragile and inflexible branches of education reaches the school. Regardless, there's no prior planning, in consideration of where what sort of school is needed or what kinds of schools merely provide fun and games. Attention to quantity still prevails over educational wisdom. And the ultimate goal of "Weststruck" education is the preparation and deposition of documents attesting to the employment value of education in the hands of persons who are able only to become the future victuals of the bureaucracy and who need documents for promotion to any position. Coordination in the business of schools just doesn't exist. Schools. We have all sorts of them: religious...secular...foreign, and schools that foster spiritual midgets and students of theology. We have technical schools and trade schools, and a legion of other kinds. But nowhere is it entered and recorded what the net result of all this variety is and why all these schools exist and what each of them fosters and for what occupations the products of these schools are being prepared.

And in the programs of all these schools there's no evidence of reliance upon tradition--no trace of the culture of the past--no relationship whatever between home and school--between society as a whole and the individual...Schools don't know what they want. But in any event, we have approximately twenty thousand new high school graduates, and on and on it'll continue ...the future victuals of all the worries and pressures and crises and insurrections. Men without faith--void of fire and enthusiasm--the listless tools of the governments of the moment, and all of them a prey. And it is because of this that the theological schools and Islamic educational centers have suddenly come to life and flourished during the past decade, since in these schools at least no one senses danger to the religious faith of the youth. However, what difference does it make since religion and irreligion and education and its lack are the problems of our cities only or are one of the amusements of city-dwellers? For, of fifty thousand villages in this country, forty-three thousand have no sort of school at all; and would that those villages that have schools didn't, since, in that case, there'd be only one, common calamity (i.e., illiteracy); whereas as it stands now, there are thousands of calamitous situations; and each place has a different one.

For instance, at the university which ought to be the most pulsating and distinguished center of research--those university institutes that have to do with technology and applied science..., at their most advanced levels of training, merely produce good

repairmen for Western manufactures. And those parts
of the university that don't concern technology and
trades, but deal rather with Islamic studies and
Iranian culture..., just as the Islamic religious
schools that foolishly assumed that they might, with
the preservation of religion and its instruction and
propagation, smother the threat of irreligion--which
is itself merely one of the symptomatic occurrences of
Weststruckness--, so the university people assumed
that they might, through refuge in Arabism and *belles
lettres*, prevent this very same danger. This is why
the Faculty of Letters and all its scholars expend
their combined energies in the exhumation of graves
and in the deep study of things past and in research
on about such-and-such and so-and-so. In such colleges,
on the one hand, a direct reaction to *Weststruckness*
can be clearly seen in this escape into ancient texts
and ancient people and the dead glories of literature
and mysticism. And on the other hand, there is here
observable the greatest and most detestable sign of
Weststruckness in the reliance on and invoking of
orientalists' words that the professors here are
guilty of...An educated and compassionate man of
traditional upbringing who is likewise a university
professor and whose spheres of interest are literature
and law studies, when he witnesses how the invasion of
the West and how industry and its techniques plunder
and carry everything away, this man--can you believe
it--supposes the more *Kalileh and Demneh* fables the
better. This is why the products of all the literature,
law, and theology faculties during the past twenty
to thirty years have been so ineffective in society
and why, in comparison with the returnees from abroad,
they seem backward and out of the main-stream. And
may God grant long lives to orientalists who compose
an encyclopedia or dictionary for every sort of
medieval poem in order to keep the products of our
colleges busy and entertained...With very few excep-
tions the products of these colleges in the past
twenty or thirty years have been esteemed scholars
the lot of whom (unfortunately) are philologists--

all of them with a smattering of knowledge about the famous--all of them idiosyncratic note writers for the margins of other people's books--all of them unravelers of lexical or historical obscurities and--all of them putting in order the graves of the known and unknown dead and demonstrating the intricacies of allusion and plagiarism...--all of them writers of articles about poets in the tenth century A.H., whose number doesn't exceed the fingers on two hands. And what's worst of all, most of these persons are teachers of literature, school administrators, and cultural leaders. From this motley group what good or blessing can be expected? Excepting greater submersion into *Weststruckness*...

A further problem is that of the horde of the European educated or the returnees from America, each and every one of them having returned a candidate for a viziership at the very least, but ending up governmental dead weight. No doubt the very existence of these individuals is a windfall. Yet observe closely and notice what sort of waste and refuse each of these treasures has proved after his return and the opening up of some spot in a ministry and his assumption of some job or other. They find neither the right environment nor have they the requisite ability--they're neither open-handed nor encouraging; and most of them aren't even sympathetic. They are perfect examples of something severed from its roots, this the result of *Weststruckness*. They are perfect specimens of individuals with their feet in the air. These are the ones who execute the notions and views of foreign advisors and experts. And contrary to the commonly accepted belief, however much the horde of returnees from abroad increases, their power to act diminishes; and the incapacity and disharmony of the organizations that have accepted the influence of the European-trained becomes greater. The reason--on the one hand--there never was a plan in sending these educated youths abroad somewhere to study something. These students, through their own prerogative and initiative, went off, each of them, to some corner of the world and studied something and gained some experience that was totally distinct and different from the experience of others. And now they've returned. And each one of them must be a cog in a wheel, a member of an enterprise, part of a government organization. Then it becomes apparent how incompatible they are and how incapable and stymied in the performance of any operation. On the other hand, each one of these young men is like a beautiful tulip or narcissus or hyacinth whose bulbs we import from Holland and nurture in the greenhouses of Tehran. And after they've bloomed, we buy a flowerpot and bear them as a gift for some friend. And even though our friend puts them in a warm room with sunlight, they don't last more than a week. These choice flowers of our society will likewise wilt from the weather of this region. We've observed them, had experience with them. And should, by chance, they not wither and die, be certain of this fact that they're compelled to go along with the tide. So, contrary to all this propaganda that is expended for the purpose of persuading those college students abroad to return home, I don't feel that the return of these students will offer the prospect of real service to the homeland till the time that an environmental setting is here made ready for their jobs of the future. What is certain is that the people who are going to turn around and advance the life and environment in this intense cold will be those who have both been nurtured in this furnace and adapted to the climate in the cooler. As long as the situation of students going to Europe remains as we see it today, with its present disharmony and the lack of coordination that exists, and as long as the matter of education in Europe is left to individual ingenuity and chance, I don't think there's much hope that the larger the horde of European educated Iranians becomes, the hope of success in the renewal of the structure of our nation will become proportionately greater.

It is because of these particulars that I feel that

the time has arrived for us to refrain from sending students to Europe and America. We have seen what results have and have not materialized from all this schooling in Europe and America. The time has arrived when we ought, according to a definite and well laid-out plan for a specific period of time, say twenty years, to send students to Japan and India for advanced (i.e., university) studies and to nowhere else. And if I propose these two countries only, it is ultimately because we know how these two countries have adapted to the machine age and how they've adopted technology and how they've coped with the problems we face. In my opinion, only in the event that such a plan is acted upon, will it be possible through the creation of an equilibrium between the Eaststruckness of future visitors to Asia and the Weststruckness of present-day returnees from Europe that one can be hopeful concerning the subject of education."

Beyond their illustration of extremes in Āl-e Aḥmad's writing career, the translations from *The Exchange of Visits* and *Weststruckness* highlight the fact that Āl-e Aḥmad's most famous book, *The School Principal* (1958), constitutes an attempt to blend fiction and social criticism, the author's skill at the former a tool for the better realization of the latter, his basic goal. Āl-e Aḥmad himself capsulizes *The School Principal* as

> the product of personal thoughts and quick, emotional judgments about the very small, but very influential domain of the school and education, accompanied, however, with explicit indications of the general conditions of the day and of this very sort of problem (i.e., illustrated in *Weststruckness*) which is destructive of independence.[3]

Thus, among the premises and criteria upon the basis of which Āl-e Aḥmad's achievement in *The School Principal* ought to be appreciated and assessed is the subordination of the art of narration to the goal of social commentary and criticism.

In this light, to observe that *The School Principal* is not a tightly knit, dramatic story involving round or developing characters or depicting concomitant and interdependent conflicts is merely to recognize that Āl-e Aḥmad is not out to create much of a story per se. Nevertheless, his skill, for example, in representing the speaking voice on the written page should not be underestimated: the first person narrator of *The School Principal*, the title character, speaks not for Āl-e Aḥmad but for himself, as a member of the very social institution his narrative indicts and not beyond censure himself. Further, the school principal's manner of recounting events in an episodic, chronological, uncomplicated, personal way, featuring, for example, the repeated use of the coordinating conjunction "and" where more exact and appropriate transition words might have been used,[4] is very natural for a narrator who is recalling events as they happened to him, just as the merging of real and imagined events in Ṣādeq Hedāyat's *The Blind Owl* (1936), Iran's most famous piece of fiction, suits and reflects the mental condition of its first person narrator.[5]

Āl-e Aḥmad's success in *The School Principal* must, thus, be measured by what the story purports to be and nothing more and nothing else. If its plot has none of the dramatic, concentrated appeal--at least after the necessary opening scene and bull sequence--of Ṣādeq Chubak's *Tangsir* (1964), still Āl-e Aḥmad avoids the occasional over-exuberance of imagery in Chubak's narrative and the disturbing, unnecessary, temporary shift of narrative point of view in the middle of *Tangsir*.[6] If the narrator of *The School Principal* fails to achieve the atmospheric drama and tension that the narrator of *The Blind Owl* realizes, Āl-e Aḥmad's singleness of narrative intent nonetheless avoids the ambiguity and shifting focus that characterizes Hedāyat's narrative. The texture of *The School Principal* is obviously not comparable to that of 'Ali Moḥammad Afghāni's monumental first novel, *Āhu Khānom's Husband* (1961); yet Āl-e Aḥmad, who sees the lack of economy as the major flaw in Afghāni's absorbing story,[7] guarantees the impact of *The School Principal* through deliberate economy and the avoidance of the romantic fallacy that *Āhu Khānom's Husband* embodies. In terms of narrative theme, Gholāmhosayn Sā'edi is more dramatically successful in *The Cannon* (1963) than is Āl-e Ahmad in *The School Principal*. In fact, in this regard, Āl-e Ahmad's own allegorical *"N" and the Pen* (1961) seems a more emphatic representation of its theme of social criticism than does the narrative of *The School Principal*.[8]

But the obvious fact remains that *The School Principal* has different goals, thus different means and consequent effects than other major works in modern Persian fiction. Whereas it may share, for example, the goal of social criticism about contemporary Iran with other narratives, one of its distinctive means is the use of a contemporary setting, not a distant, historical one as in *"N" and the Pen*. In this light, *The School Principal* is like Bozorg 'Alavi's *Her Eyes* (1951), the serious shortcomings of the latter novel—it has had an uncritical yet understandable popularity in some circles in Iran—illustrating, by way of contrast, some positive aspects of *The School Principal*.[9]

'Alavi's narrative is, first, melodramatic, all its characters, including a frustrated lover who commits suicide, presented in terms of superlatives: the narrator is superlatively faithful to the memory of the dead painter, Mākān, and superlatively patient in his quest to discover whose eyes are represented in one of Mākān's portraits; the woman whose eyes they are is superlatively wealthy, beautiful, and unhappy; the dead Mākān is superlatively superior as a human being. None of these characters is convincingly motivated. At the very core of Āl-e Ahmad's narrative on the other hand, there is real motivation, much of it the very basis of Āl-e Ahmad's social criticism: the motivation that causes schools to be built, that leads teachers to teach, students to study, and principals become principals.

Secondly, 'Alavi preaches through his characters, gratuitously asserting that the novel's narrator and the heroine are prompted to recount and record their connections with the dead Mākān because of their realization that the fruits of such a labor will inspire Iranian youths of today. By way of contrast, in *The School Principal*, beyond the clear distinction between the writer and his narrator, there is a consistent and maintained interest in the realistic portrayal of the narrator's speaking voice and in the realistic narration of events, the very impact of the story arising from the baldness and uneditorialized nature of the presentation, this impact leading an early reviewer of *The School Principal* to remark, almost apologetically:

> Āl-e Aḥmad describes a school principal who is psychologically unfit for the job he has. The problems he encounters in the Education Department milieu torture him and intensify his pessimism and oblige him, for the purpose of executing the duties of his position, occasionally to commit actions he ought not to. In this story, some embarrassing and shameful facts are recounted which, it is unfortunately necessary to admit, represent an aspect of truth.[10]

Thirdly, unlike Āl-e Aḥmad who sees clearly that the nature of his materials and the effect he wishes them to have on the reader require a first person narrator, 'Alavi does not foresee the potential unsuitability, lifelessness, and improbability that a first person narrator lends to his materials and, thus, besides not distinguishing between the speaking voices of his narrator and the novel's heroine who tells her story within the frame of the narrator's recounting of events, obliges his narrator to relate events to which the narrator was not a witness and about which he apparently could not later have been totally apprised.[11]

In short, as the foregoing implies, *The School Principal*, with its economy, straightforwardness, and singleness of purpose, holds a unique place in modern Persian fiction. It is not Iran's most moving novel, which distinction probably belongs to Ṣādeq Chubak's *The Patient Stone* (1967), a grim, naturalistic tableau, in multiple stream of consciousness technique, of the lives of five or six people in Shirāz some forty years ago.[12] In fact, it is in comparison with *The Patient Stone*, in which the plot is likewise of secondary importance, that the basic flatness of Āl-e Aḥmad's characters becomes accentuated. For in *The Patient Stone*, even the hapless child Kākolzari has depth of personality and unwitting vision, and the main speaker, Aḥmad *Āqā* is almost philosophic in his musings and private conversations. Āl-e Aḥmad's characters, however, are nameless, their roles the representation of their function in the educational *milieu*, and nothing more. And if this lack of depth and roundness in character portrayal may be considered the chief reason for the failure of *The School Principal* to affect reader emotion as does *The Patient Stone*, it seems to be no accidental lack, but rather the author's intentional limiting of focus for the purpose of social criticism, in which his goal is not to capture hearts, but to capture minds and, perhaps, persuade those minds to a course of action. In a sense, then, Āl-e Aḥmad's achievement in *The School Principal* must be evaluated as a fictional argument intended to convince its readers of a truth about a segment of Iranian society. As such, it may be a very familiar fictional form for readers of sociological and protest fiction in Europe and America during the past hundred years, to whom *The School Principal* may seem a bland indictment of the Iranian elementary education milieu in comparison with social protest classics such as Upton Sinclair's *The Jungle* and

John Steinbeck's *The Grapes of Wrath*. But at its publication, *The School Principal* stood almost alone in modern Persian fiction. As one critic puts it, *The School Principal* "is the first of its kind in Iran. It is a (semi-)autobiographical work, with contemporary setting, contemporary characters and contemporary issues."[13]

One piece of Persian fiction comparable in more than a superficial way to *The School Principal* is Āl-e Aḥmad's last novel, *The Cursing of the Land* (1968), a translation of the opening scene of which here follows for the purpose of rounding out this introduction to *The School Principal* and the place it holds in Āl-e Aḥmad's career as a writer and in modern Persian literature:

The Cursing of the Land[14]

"Alright, then. Here it is, the village. I got here yesterday afternoon. The principal had lined up the kids and brought them along to meet me. Twenty, thirty of them. In the middle of the village square. Its name?...*Ḥasan-Ābād* or *Hosayn-Ābād* or *'Ali-Ābād*. It's perfectly obvious. The name, it's not important. A village like all villages. One mud beehive, human-being size. Next to a stream or a spring or a pool or a *qanāt*. In other words, an *ābādī*. With this difference that I was a gym teacher in one, and in another, a math teacher. And now, here, I'm to be the teacher of the fifth grade, which was opened this year and the running of which is out of the hands of the natives. I don't have any idea why they don't let me stay in the city schools. It's been five years since I got out of Teachers' Training School, and the whole time I've spent in half-baked villages. Maybe I myself have wanted it this way?... No. It's got to be that there's something engraved on this forehead of mine."

As this brief excerpt intimates, *The Cursing of the Land* is, in terms of narrative point of view, a continuation of *The School Principal*. In both novels,

) 23 (

the reader meets a narrator already imbued with either cynicism or what might be called an unsympathetic realism resulting from experiences prior to and outside of the narrative context. But whereas the narrator of *The School Principal* has moments when the reader can sympathize and almost identify with him, the narrator of *The Cursing of the Land* exhibits almost no chinks in his armor of cynicism. It is as if in the course of development of sharper focus in his war against social ills, Āl-e Aḥmad becomes, in the period between *The School Principal* (1958) and *The Cursing of the Land* (1968), more impatient in his desire for reader awareness of and attention to the seriousness of these problems and thus feels less constrained to take pains to give plausible and entertaining fictional form to his exposé in *The Cursing of the Land*. This seems to be one reason why *The Cursing of the Land*, though richer in detail, characterization, and narrative conflict than *The School Principal*, may seem a less effective (plausible) piece of fictional social criticism. A second reason is the wider scope of social criticism in *The Cursing of the Land*. In *The School Principal*, the subject is the educational system and very little is presented that somehow does not reach back to the school. But in *The Cursing of the Land*, where the geographical focus is a village, the social problems treated include aspects of land reform, mechanization, education, and military conscription, the picture of life being comprehensively negative, the reader eventually feeling that some of the action has been contrived to create such a wholly negative situation. Of course, this is a possible charge against *The School Principal* and much social protest fiction in general.

The Cursing of the Land is the last of Āl-e Aḥmad's major published writings. Among them, *The Exchange of Visits* (1946) announced Āl-e Aḥmad to the Iranian literary world as a writer of promise. *The School Principal* (1958) represented the fulfillment of this promise and demonstrated that Āl-e Ahmad had determined to be a writer of the Iranian present and not of the grand and timeless issues, such as Hedāyat and Chubak. And *"N" and the Pen, Weststruckness,* and *The Cursing of the Land* reaffirmed this and broadened the scope of Āl-e Ahmad's social criticism.

With the publication of *The School Principal* (1958), Āl-e Ahmad became a major spokesman for the nonestablishment Iranian intelligentsia, a role he held unchallenged till his death in 1969. Sādeq Hedāyat, whose troubled life ended in a Paris suicide in 1951, had previously been a spokesman for the intelligentsia, but in an aesthetic, romantic sense and not as a standard bearer in a war against social ills. Āl-e Ahmad seems to have been aware of his particular appeal. In 1965, he observed in a recorded discussion that he was happy to have found an audience merely by writing, "since Hedāyat to achieve this had to commit suicide. But I have been able, without resorting to such a romantic antic, to affect people."[15] And on another occasion, again comparing his approach to Hedāyat's, Āl-e Ahmad asserts that general understanding of the role of modern Persian fiction as a voice for social commentary is so pervasive that no longer can a writer, as Hedāyat did in *The Blind Owl,* proclaim that his is writing merely for his shadow on the wall.[16]

Being a spokesman and social critic impatient for change lay a great responsibility on Āl-e Ahmad that he was not always up to shouldering. His strong sense of nationalism, concomitant iconoclasm, and sometimes anti-Western sentiments are, simultaneously, the strength and weakness of his writing. On the one hand, they imbue his prose with force, bite, and sincerity. On the other, they persuade him, on occasion, to alter facts to suit his argument.[17] Massud Farzān argues that Āl-e Ahmad "is not a chauvinist or traditionalist. What he seems to be after is a brutal search after social and cultural truths, and a daring determination to put them in the light for the

) 25 (

literate public. He is an iconoclast who defies well-established beliefs without reservation."[18]

If this is a fair judgment, it means either that Āl-e Aḥmad's ability to gather and discern facts was sometimes deficient or that his determination to expose social ills gave him, in his own view, a rhetorical right to exaggerate for the sake of the truth he sought to put before his readers.

What all this means for the reader of *The School Principal* is that he must exercise two different sorts of judgment in assessing the book. First, because *The School Principal* is fiction, critical judgment as to the plausibility of events stemming from initial premises (such as the personality the narrator brings to the story) and as to the success of the story-telling and as prose suited to the narrator's personality and condition, must be exercised. Second, because Āl-e Aḥmad's implicit aim in *The School Principal*, made explicit by him in an article quoted from above, is to reveal problems existing in the Iranian educational system and periphery, several questions must be asked: Do Āl-e Aḥmad's fictional events have an air of reality about them? Are there any means by which readers who have no experience of the Iranian educational system can check the veracity of Āl-e Aḥmad's fictional argument? Do the conditions Āl-e Aḥmad depicts describe the situation today, some sixteen years later, during which time under the aegis of the Shah's White Revolution educational reforms have been called for? There are no persuasive, objective data or statistics with which to demonstrate the accuracy and veracity of Āl-e Aḥmad's account or to prove the assertion that things have changed in the last sixteen years. The only answer to any of these questions may lie in citing one probable reason for the popularity of *The School Principal*,[19] that being the feeling of many readers that the book mirrors pieces of truths and real, recognizable situations similar to what they themselves have experienced. And obviously, the interest which many foreigners in Iran may have in *The School Principal* lies in the feeling that there is truth in the novel which can help inspire positive action and reform. And now two English translations of *The School Principal* are being readied for publication, the first by John K. Newton, which this essay prefaces, of which excerpts have appeared in the Peace Corps *Volunteer* magazine, and the second by Professor Gidhari Tikku, reportedly to be published in the Persian Heritage Series.

Both translations bespeak a conviction that an audience wider than the Persian-speaking one should be apprised of the realities which *The School Principal* fictionally depicts, this audience including the many foreigners involved directly or indirectly in education in Iran and, more broadly, those individuals interested in the particulars of the human condition everywhere, to which another audience might be added: people who are international in their taste for imaginative literature. For *The School Principal*, whatever it is finally judged to be as a social document, is assuredly one of the dozen or so major pieces of fiction in contemporary Persian literature.

When Jalāl Āl-e Aḥmad died at forty-six of a heart attack in September, 1969, his following whispered that he had not died of a heart attack. And shortly after Jalāl's death, most of his works became unobtainable in bookstores, the first of these to become available again, *The Exchange of Visits*, appearing in a new edition in mid-November, 1970; *The School Principal* was reissued in May, 1971; and *"N" and the Pen*, *Weststruckness*, and *The Cursing of the Land*, among others, are still unavailable at this writing. It seems most probable that Jalāl did die of a heart attack and that the rumor his followers nurtured was a symptom both of the anti-establishment feelings he and his followers share and of the pessimism, suspicion, and cynicism that characterize the Iranian intelligentsia. And there seem to be two possible explanations for the disappearance of Āl-e Aḥmad's works right after his death and for the delay in the publication of new editions. First, perhaps the executors of Jalāl's will decided to reissue his works one at a time over a protracted period for financial reasons. Or, second, perhaps the Iran government saw fit after Jalāl's death to let things cool off a bit by keeping his books out of circulation, this decision an indication of the significance and presumed impact of a book such as *The School Principal*.

The truth of the matter is probably a combination of both conjectures, the second of which is something of an indication of the courage of Āl-e Ahmad who, as a writer, tread a tight-rope during a twenty-four year career, saying as much of what he thought was the truth as he could short of incurring censorship. Jalāl's persistence as a social critic surely cost him in material success and peace of mind. One may not happen to agree with the pessimism and cynicism that are reflected in much of Āl-e Ahmad's writing, but one has to admire any man who has a conscience and speaks from it.

As a final note, I feel obliged to admit an initial uncertainty about the most appropriate way in which to introduce John Newton's translation of *The School Principal*, which is the best English translation of any piece of Persian, medieval or modern, that I have ever read. The large number of English speaking foreigners living in Iran deserve one or more sorts of introduction. For students and scholars of Middle Eastern and Iranian affairs another approach is called for. And comparative literature devotees could expect a distinctive treatment. The course I have chosen, with some hesitation, is to introduce *The School Principal* to non-specialists.

In any case, I thank John Newton, former roommate and ever kindred spirit, for inviting me to introduce his translation and to prepare the backnotes for terms and expressions, italicized in the text, needing some explanation for readers with no knowledge of the Persian language and Iranian culture.

Michael Craig Hillmann
The University of Texas at Austin
August, 1974

NOTES--INTRODUCTION

[1] Jalāl Āl-e Ahmad, "Goldān-e Chini," *Did-o Bāzdid*, 4th ed. (Tehran: Amir Kabir, 1970), pp. 71-78.
[2] Idem, "Farhang va Dāneshgāh Cheh Mikonand," *Gharbzadegi* (Tehran, 1962), pp. 94-99.
[3] Idem, "Masalan Sharh-e Ahvālāt," *Jahān-e Now* 24 (1969), no. 3: 7. In this article, Āl-e Ahmad traces his education, teaching, writing, and editorial careers, and his membership in the now defunct Iranian Tudeh Communist party.
[4] Mohammad 'Ali Jamālzādeh, "Modir-e Madraseh," *Rāhnemā-ye Ketāb* 1 (1958): 168. Jamālzādeh also notes the narrator's frequent use of elliptic sentences (p. 170), a feature of narrative style very suited to the character and situation of the narrator.
[5] *Buf-e Kur* has been translated into English by J.P. Costello, *The Blind Owl* (London: Calder/New York: Grove, 1957) and by Iraj Bashiri, *Hedayat's Ivory Tower* (Minneapolis: Manor House, 1974). Of Costello's translation, Massud Farzan, "Modern Persian Literature: How Good Is It?" *University of Pennsylvania--Pahlavi University Lecture Series* (Spring, 1966), p. 12, asserts: "Undoubtedly the English translation of this book has done it great injustice." The same holds true for Bashiri's translation, which is accompanied by a curious "structural analysis." In any case, Peter W. Avery's still unpublished translation may hopefully, when published, give English-speaking readers a fairer sense of the original, which well deserves its reputation as a most provocative piece of modern Persian fiction.

[6]Ṣādeq Chubak, *Tangsir*, 2nd ed. (Tehran: Jāvidān, 1968), pp. 151-54, where the otherwise unidentified, but patently autobiographical pronoun "I" intrudes temporarily to recount Moḥammad's passing by. The whole novel, based upon a basically true story popular in the south of Iran and previously told by Rasul Parvizi in "Shir Moḥammad," *Shalvārhā-ye Vaṣleh-dār* (1957), exists in an unpublished English translation which will hopefully be someday published.

[7]Āl-e Aḥmad, *Arzyābi-ye Shetābzadeh* (Tabriz: Ebn-e Sinā, 1965), p. 72.

[8]Ibid., pp. 93 and 100, where Āl-e Ahmad declares that his use of the *yaki bud yaki nabud* ("once upon a time") story-telling mode and of an allegorical, historical setting in *"N" and the Pen* was deliberate, political circumstances dictating his decision. In *Weststruckness*, p. 23, Āl-e Aḥmad asserts that *"N" and the Pen* depicts the effects historically consequent upon the official linking of church and state at the advent of the Ṣafavid dynasty in A.D. 1499, whereupon Persian society proved itself unwilling any longer to suffer for principles and ideals but preferred thereafter to pay lip service to past heroes and martyrs instead. In "Maṣalan Sharḥ-e Aḥvālāt," p. 7, Āl-e Aḥmad asserts that *"N" and the Pen* portrays the causes of the defeat of the leftist movements in Iran after World War II, his choice of an historical setting dictated by a desire to avoid official censoring of the book. Lack of space forbids the inclusion of a translated section from *"N" and the Pen* here, despite the fact that it may be Āl-e Aḥmad's best piece of fiction, having, as well, its artistic and formal roots in a native Iranian tradition, unlike nearly all other major pieces of recent Persian fiction which naturally enough owe something of form and techniques to Western models.

[9]The setting of *Her Eyes*, if not exactly contemporary, i.e., the reign of Reẓā Shāh who was deposed in 1941, is nevertheless qualitatively contemporary in the same sense that "The China Flowerpot" reflects contemporary attitudes. For a brief discussion of *Her*

Eyes, see Hasan Kāmshād, *Modern Persian Pros Literature* (Cambridge: University Press, 1966), pp. 120-24. Kāmshād's study, by the way, is the only available lengthy treatment in English of modern Persian prose literature; it is superficial and exhibits critical inaccuracies and imbalance of treatment (e.g., two pages are devoted to Āl-e Aḥmad and five to Ṣan-'atizādeh Kermāni), but is nevertheless useful as a checklist of major Persian prose works from the translation into Persian of James Morier's *The Adventures of Ḥaji Baba of Ispahan* in 1905 to the publication of Afghāni's *The Husband of Āhu Khānom* in 1961 and for its bibliography of secondary sources and translations of Persian prose works. Kāmshād's favorable impression of *Her Eyes* is an example of the uncritical nature of some of his evaluations.

[10]"Modir-e Madraseh," *Rāhnemā-ye Ketāb* 1 (1958): 119. Jamālzādeh, "Modir-e Madraseh," p. 174, concurs with this judgment of the veracity of Āl-e Aḥmad's social criticism and observes that the chief success of *The School Principal* lies in Āl-e Aḥmad's comprehensive realism and total avoidance of the sentimental and melodramatic.

[11]Bozorg 'Alavi, *Chashmhāyash*, 2nd ed. (Tehran, 1962), p. 21: the interview between Khaltāsh and Mākān; p. 25: Mākān's sleepless nights on the roof of his house.

[12]Ṣādeq Chubak, *Sang-e Ṣabūr* (Tehran: Jāvidān 'Elmi, 1967). The stream of consciousness technique so successfully employed in this novel may owe less to European and American models than to Hedāyat's "Buried Alive," "Three Drops of Blood," and *The Blind Owl*. As successful a piece of fiction as it is, Chubak's *The Patient Stone* is not without its flaws, two of which, as noted by Reẓā Barāheni, *Qessehnevisi*, 2nd ed. (Tehran: Ashrafi, 1969), pp. 680-82, are the inclusion of a section from Ferdowsi's *Shāhnāmeh* in one of Aḥmad Āqā's monologues (pp. 99-114) and the playlet at the novel's end (pp. 326-400), both sections unintegrated into the novel and of dubious artistic merit in their own right.

[13] Farzān, "Persian Literature," p. 15.
[14] Āl-e Aḥmad, *Nefrin-e Zamin* (Tehrān: Nil, 1968).
[15] Āl-e Aḥmad, *Arzyābi*, p. 73.
[16] Ibid., p. 61.
[17] For example, in *Kārnāmeh-ye Seh Sāleh* (Tehran: Nil, 1968), p. 102, Āl-e Aḥmad asserts that as of 1968 there were nine hundred American Peace Corps volunteers working in Iranian villages, each of them paid five to seven dollars a day and each provided with a translator, their service serving as training for future employment in the United States Department of State. But according to Roger Wangsness, the Program-Training Administrative Officer for the Peace Corps in Iran in the Spring of 1971, less than three hundred Peace Corps volunteers were serving in Iran in 1968, only a small number of whom worked in villages, none of whom was ever provided with a formal translator. The approximate daily salary for these volunteers was $3.50, in addition to which housing was provided, directly or indirectly, by the Iranian agency to which the volunteers were assigned. These volunteers were eligible to apply for employment with the Department of State once their Peace Corps service ended, but only in the same terms as other qualified American citizens; and in applying for such employment, these ex-volunteers could not expect to be assigned to Iran.
[18] Farzān "Persian Literature," p. 16.
[19] Āl-e Aḥmad, *Arzyābi*, notes several facts that must be borne in mind when considering the "popularity" of a piece of contemporary Persian fiction. First, no Iranian writer of interpretive fiction has yet been able to earn a living through his craft (pp.62-63). Second, interpretive fiction is still a relatively young and experimental craft in Iran (p. 66) unable to compete in terms of popularity with Persian translations of Western classics and bestsellers or with the works of Iranian hack and escape fiction writers. Third, a serious writer who chooses an independent stance faces a prospect of isolation (p. 86).

THE SCHOOL PRINCIPAL

1

As I passed through the door, cigarette in hand, I had to force myself to say hello. For no reason at all, I felt like acting tough. Having granted me permission to sit, the local Chief of Education glanced for a lingering second at my hand and went about finishing what he had been writing. After I placed a copy of the order on his desk, he directed his attention my way. Neither of us said a word. He thumbed through the order along with its attached papers, sucked in his chin, and then relaxed. With an air of serenity as if free of all anger, he said: "We have no openings, Āqā." Then, an outburst:
> "What's going on around here? Everyday they stick an order in somebody's hand and tell him to look me up...Yesterday I told the Director General..."

I didn't feel like listening to this nonsense, so I cut him off: "May I request that Your Excellency kindly put that in writing at the bottom of the sheet?" At the same time I flicked my cigarette ashes into the gleaming ashtray on his desk. The desk top was immaculate. Just like a bridal suite. Everything in its place. Not one speck of dust. Only the ashes from my cigarette. Like spit on a freshly shaven face... He picked up his pen, wrote something beneath the order, signed it, and out I went. Finished.

I couldn't take much of this fellow. It was obvious from the way he talked that he had just recently been appointed chief. He had a forced air of pomposity about him and spoke slowly into your eyes. You'd think that ears weren't necessary in order to hear him. I had laid out 150 *tomans* in the Central Personnel Department to get this paper signed and had even brought recommendations. For two months now I had been chasing around. My papers were absolutely impeccable. Whether he liked it or not, I knew that the matter was closed. And he knew it too. Certainly he also realized that with all these protestations he had only made himself look more foolish. But what was done was done.

All of this had come about because they had suggested in the Central Personnel Department that for formality's sake I ought to take a copy of the order to show the Chief. After all, who could overrule an order from the Central Personnel Department? This was a Ministry and a Central Personnel Department. No joking matter. I had been absolutely certain that I wouldn't need to resort to this line of reasoning. All the blame for this latest holdup I placed on the damn cigarette which, in my mind's eye, I'd envisioned paying for out of the overtime pay from my new job.

Of course, I was utterly nauseated with teaching; ten years of teaching abc's to the blank, gaping faces of the people's children, all of it the stupidest nonsense you can possibly imagine...*esteghnā'* is spelled with the letter *ghayn* and *esteqrā'* with *qaf* and the Khorāsān and the Indian styles of poetry and the oldest poem in Persian and devices like anadiplosis and proverbial figures of speech...and similar such crap. I realized I was turning into a donkey. One day I said to myself: I should become a principal. A grade school principal. I won't teach another class. My conscience will no longer incessantly vascillate between giving out a C or a C+ and I won't need to give every idiot a high enough grade to escape from wasting my time in the repeat examinations and thus preserve for myself the most delightful days of the entire summer, the last few days of vacation. Here lay the root of my motivation. I went out and asked somebody with the inside dope, a go-between who could fix it up for me. He arranged things with the Central Personnel Department, extracting promises, making agreements, and organizing a lobby of supporters. Then, one day, they gave me the address of a school to check out to see if it suited me or not. And off I went.

It was a two story school, newly built, standing alone at the foot of the mountain, facing the sun. Some filthy-rich philanthropist had put up the building in the middle of his own property and placed it at the disposal of the Office of Education for twenty-five years in hopes that they'd make a school out of it, that the area might be frequented, that roads might be pounded out, and the whole scheme would grow and grow and continue to develop, until all the mommies and daddies in town came out, bought up the land, and built homes around the school so their kids wouldn't have to travel so far to get there. By that time his land would have shot up from one *'abbāsi* per meter to 100 *tomans*. This character had even had his name tiled into the wall in fine stylized writing on a blue background surrounded by decorative squiggles and swirls. Of course the school was named after him as well. So far no neighbors had been found to argue among themselves, pull out their favorite lines from *Sa'di* and *Bābā Ṭāher,* and pound another page from the history of poets into the *kucheh* wall.

The school's sign was a beauty, large and legible. From 150 meters away it screamed out the motto, "Power is...whatever you want it to be," with the national symbol of the lion standing up there on three legs, trying to maintain his balance, with joined eyebrows, sword in hand, and lady sun riding piggyback. A stone's throw from the school on all sides was the desert--limitless, waterless and desolate. On the end facing north, a row of pines which had collapsed on top of each other rose up over a mud garden wall, staining the sky with long dark spots. Certainly before twenty-five years were up, this whole area would be filled with the blare of car horns, the commotion of children playing, the shouts of beet sellers, the bells of news dealers, and cries of "I have fresh cucumbers." This fellow indeed had it made. You know perhaps he bought this whole thing for not more than ten or twelve *shāhis*. Maybe he even registered the land just as it is. Um?

Yes sir. I had these very thoughts on that day I dropped in on the school incognito. But, in the end, I came to the conclusion that people do indeed have the right to feather their own nests. I said to myself, "If you're a man, use your brains and become principal of this very school." And so I had pursued the matter until it had reached this stage.

On the same day as my inspection tour, I discovered that the former principal was in jail. Surely he had been a suspected communist sympathizer and, just as surely, was now atoning for sins either he had never committed or the proverbial *blacksmith in Balkh* had. Among the paper dolls hanging around the Chief of Education, there wasn't a single soul prepared to exert the necessary effort to secure the principal's position and collect the subsequent raise. The job didn't have the special post allowance for out-of-the-way places. I had obtained this information from the Personnel Department. Letter-written apologies weren't in fashion yet, so I had no reason to anticipate this fellow's early release from the clink. And I couldn't think of anyone else who would be all that excited about coming out here in the middle of nowhere with its rugged winters and transportation problems. This put my mind at ease. And besides, the Central Personnel Department had agreed.

It's true, until the smell of money arose, they had found a few faults with me, and some legal technicalities. For example, they all said there has to be something in it for this guy that doesn't meet the eye. Why else would he, meaning me, with ten years of teaching experience, want to be a grade school principal? According to their interpretations, I had to be out of my mind to choose to wash my hands of as honorable and as important a vocation as teaching. Or maybe I was a pederast, a child molester, or some other kind of pervert. Stuff like that.

This was as far as my hopes had got until the go-between made it clear that I'd have to "loosen a few purse strings." And so I did. In those days the monthly expense account of 150 *tomans* which went with the position of principal was no small piece of change I could overlook. And if I did overlook it, then what? I'd have to return to those classes, those compositions, and those readings, Nezāmi's *The Four Discourses* and Kaykāvus' *A Mirror for Princes* the school yearbook and all the rest of that crap.

All this persuaded me to go straight back from the Chief of Education to the Central Personnel Department and on into the office of my agent. I threw the copy of the order down in front of him, told him what had transpired, and walked out. Two days later, when I returned, it was obvious that my guess had been correct. The Chief of Education had said, "I don't want any of these arrogant university graduates who go cigarette in hand into any room they please." And my guy had answered, "Oh, never, absolutely not!...Such and such is this way and he's that way and indeed, he's altogether totally different than the others." On and on with this b.s. I was advised to put my mind at ease and go see the Chief again next Thursday...I did.

This time he stood up to greet me. "I say, *Āqā*,... Why didn't you tell me?"...After exchanging pleasantries and smiles, he ordered tea, complained about his staff, and, in his own words, "briefed" me on the local situation. Then he delivered me to the school in his own car, ordered the bell rung early, and, in the presence of all the teachers and the *nāzem*, went into a long oration about the characteristics of the new principal, meaning me. He then departed, and there I was with one newly-founded six-year grade school, one nāzem, seven teachers, and two-hundred thirty-five students. I had indeed become a genuine, bona fide grade school principal.

2

The nāzem was a strapping young man who spoke in a loud voice. Giving commands and shouting prohibitions came easily to him, and he had a real knack for yelling "Come here!" and "Get over there!" He was in so thick with the bigger kids that they pretty much ran the school themselves. It was obvious they could do without the interference of a third party like myself, and that without a principal, the school was running just fine.

The teacher of the fourth grade was an incredibly obese fellow. Half of him was enough to make one ordinary man. He was the first thing in the office that caught my eye; one of those who, if you saw him in the street, you'd swear he was the Director General. He spoke formal textbook Persian for which reason perhaps, after the Chief of Education had left and taken all his welcoming ceremony with him, he was the one to extend congratulations on behalf of his colleagues and to point out that "God willing, next year, under Your Excellency's protective shadow, we shall also have high school classes." Clearly, little by little, this fellow was becoming too big for a grade school, in more ways than one. While he talked I wondered how in the world anyone could develop a figure like this and dress in such a splendid fashion on a meagre teacher's wage. Then and there I made up my mind that starting tomorrow, I was going to shave everyday, wear a clean collar, and keep my trouser creases pressed.

The first grade teacher was a slight, dark-skinned man with an unshaven face, a close-cropped head and a

buttoned shirt collar, with no necktie, in the old-
fashioned way. He looked like one of those scribes who
sit around the post office writing letters for
illiterates--or like somebody's servant. He was a quiet
man and had a right to be. One might guess that such
a fellow dared speak only when he was in front of the
first grade, and even then only about long "a" and
short "e." The second grade teacher was short and
squat. Instead of speaking, he squeaked and one of his
eyes was crossed. That first day, whenever he spoke, I
couldn't figure out who or what he was looking at. With
every little squeak, he giggled. Obviously he was the
laughing stock of his colleagues who thought of him as
entertainment for during classbreaks. My heart bled for
the poor kids--how could they possibly sit quietly in a
classroom with a teacher like this? The third grade
teacher was a slender youth, tall and clean shaven, with
a bony face and a high starched collar. When he walked,
one couldn't be certain his feet wouldn't suddenly
cross and pitch him onto his face. But, like a top,
he somehow managed to keep spinning. When he spoke,
his words came out in choppy bursts, which is to say, in
staccato. His larynx didn't have a capacity of more
than three words. He eyes had a weird shine to them
that wasn't just from intelligence. Something
unhealthy in their shine persuaded me to question the
nāẓem, if he were tubercular. Of course he didn't have
T.B., but was rather a poor boy from the provinces,
who lived alone and who, in addition to teaching, was
studying at the university. The fifth and sixth grades
were run by two people together. The one who taught
Persian, religious law, history and geography,
handicrafts, and similar diversions was a
youngster with slicked down, Brylcreemed hair,
tight-cuffed trousers, a pocket handkerchief and a
wide yellow tie, which was tacked down on his chest by
an anchor-shaped pin. He was forever touching up the
sides of his hair with his hand and glacing at himself
in the mirror. The other, who taught arithmetic,
investment and interest, and some other stuff, was a

grave and solemn youngster, who looked to be from the Caspian Sea region. He had confidence in himself and was the only teacher who carried cigarettes in his pocket. He was obviously successful in class. Besides these, we also had a gym teacher, whom I met two weeks later. He was one of those A.W.O.L.'s from Isfahan, absent three days every week, and, when he was around, was always bitching.

It was with people like this that I had to begin work and, with their help, run a school. Watching over and educating two hundred thirty-five children was a task no easier than completing the first trial of *Rostam*. But for someone like myself, who had flown from the teaching cage, any place I landed would be heaven and any job, my heart's desire. This was what had got me to dress up in my finest and fly to the edge of the abyss.

Once the Chief of Education left, I tried to ingratiate myself with the teachers, warmly inquiring after everyone's health and welfare. Then I offered everyone a cigarette. This was the foundation for cooperation and fellow feeling. I was glad I would have the opportunity to become acquainted with these new people, gain access to their inner-most secrets, and open the closed doors to their private worlds. I asked each one individually how work was going, and how life was treating them. Only the third grade teacher went to the university. The one with the anchor on his chest studied English every night in hopes of going to America. Two of them had wives: the "post office scribe" of the first grade, and the "Director General" of the fourth. There being no arrangements for tea or anything, during the fifteen minute breaks, they simply gathered together in the office and showed one another that once again they had survived yet another class unscathed. And then it started all over again. This couldn't continue. One should observe all the amenities. I stuck my hand into my pocket and forked out a five *toman* bill. It was resolved that a brazier would be set up and that they'd fix their own tea. The one with the crossed eyes was delegated for this responsibility. After that the bell rang. The kids lined up and the *nāzem*, at the door's edge, impatiently swayed from foot to foot. He seemed about to say something when the "Director General" arrived to help, the latter obviously knowing that with his appearance he could butt in anywhere and into any problem. He gestured to me that it wouldn't be a bad idea for me to say a few words to the group. Personally, I wasn't at all opposed to the idea. The *nāzem* explained to the children what was going on, and as I came forward they burst into applause. All of their heads had been shaved clean, some of them had white collars pinned to their coats, and almost all were wearing *giveh* shoes. The clothes on ten or twelve fairly cried out in protest against the bodies they were so illsuited to adorn. Rags passed on by fathers and big brothers. The "bear's leftovers for the hyena!" A little red-haired fellow who was standing in the third grade line was trying to conceal a huge rent in his coat pocket; the sixth graders were all chattering in each other's ears, and in the rear of the first grade line, two or three of them were wiping their runny noses with their coat sleeves when I suddenly appeared before them. I really hadn't a thing to say. I can only recall now that I pointed out something about how the new principal, meaning me, really had wished to have one of them for his own offspring, but now that he had all of them he wasn't quite sure how to proceed. They were all giggling under their breath and one of them in the middle of the back rows let loose with a guffaw. Suddenly it hit me that in order to get anything across to children, you need a special approach. Afterwards, a cold chill shot through me. 'This is going to be no picnic, my friend!' Before, I'd thought I could simply go to my office, close the door behind me, and, free from the headaches of running a class, proceed with my own work. I'd thought that in the *nāzem* I had

somebody to take care of the work and that a system
had already been set up which required no interference on my part. But now I saw that it wasn't going
to be that simple. If tomorrow one of them cracked
another in the head and broke it, if one of them got
run over by a car, if one of them fell off the porch,
what on earth could I do? I can't remember anymore
what I said to them. All I can remember is that when
the bell finally rang and the lines headed off to
class, I had broken out in a sweat. I paced up and
down on the porch until the teachers all hustled off
to class, and then I went inside.

The *nāẓem* and I were then alone. The door opened a
crack and something slid softly in. It was a person--
the school janitor with his peasant face, unshaven
beard, and short stature. He walked with a clumping
straddle-legged gait and kept his arms away out from
his sides. When he talked he panted, as if he'd
just finished a foot race. He came in, stood by the
edge of the door, and looked me straight in the eye.
I asked him how he was. Whatever condition he was in,
he was prepared to submit full attesting evidence.
He had a ninety *toman* a month salary, a wife and a
child who, you can be sure, had more than an ample
number of playmates. They'd given him the storeroom
next to the outhouse. But he had yet to collect his
five *toman* monthly fee for janitorial services. In
this state of affairs, he'd purchased a pair of rugs
on an installment plan for 350 *tomans*--200 of which
were yet to be paid. In one minute's time he poured
out all his grievances. When his supplications were
finished, I sent him off to fix some tea. The *nāẓem*
said he was one of the villagers from the estate of
the school's landlord, that the Office of Education
had hired him at the landlord's behest, and that one
entire article in the lease agreement transferring
the school building to the Office of Education pertained specifically to him. Obviously, he, his wife,
and his child were all part of the school's "dowry."
I had personally experienced that "maids who come as

) 44 (

part of the dowry" soon prove to be nuisances. When I
said this very thing to the nāẓem, he began to pour
out his own grievances; about "what an ingrate this
fellow was, how brazen, and how up till now he'd stood
hundreds of times right among the teachers..." and on
and on with these kinds of faults and deviations.
Then I turned to the nāẓem himself. The year before
he'd got out of normal school. He'd worked one year
in Garmsar and Karaj and this year had arrived here.
His father had two wives. From the first one, he had
two sons, both of whom had turned out to be thugs,
and from the second, only the nāẓem had been interested in studying and had made a name for himself.
He supported his sick mother and had heard no news
from his father for years; and worst of all were the
expenses for drugs and medicine...They had gotten a
room for fifty-five tomans a month, and his salary
of one hundred fifty tomans barely sufficed. If he
could just push himself a little further, in three
years time he would be able to benefit from the extra
wages given for maintaining school discipline...
Afterwards, I got up to inspect the classes.
   The second class was next to the office and, at
that moment, the children were struggling to add 754
to 261. Their cross-eyed teacher seemed to be signal-
ling to the third desk while heading towards the
first. Next came the auditorium--big and empty, with
most of its space taken up by two white, four-cornered
pillars. In the back on one side were three broken
benches. The wall opposite was covered with pictures
of various champions, boxers, wrestlers, black runners
and Egyptian weight lifters. A huge map of Asia "presented by 'Ali Mardān, the Hindi, to the grammar
school" on behalf of the manufacturing company whose
trademark was printed at the bottom covered the
wall on the right. It was drawn by an unskilled hand.
The blue of the seas looked like a dead man's saliva,
and the Caspian Sea resembled a feathered aigrette. A:
the railroad lines were embossed and they extended fr(
one end of the country to the other, even down past

Kermān. The Indonesian islands were in one long strip,
with Singapore fastened to the end. Each little piece
at the bottom of the map was done in a different hue--
a collection of every conceivable color, like a
traveler's blanket roll containing forty different
colored items. All the borders could be clearly
distinguished by emblems of national independence,
armies, insignias, coins, stamps, and this and that
blustering claim of power and strength. Each one of
them was under the thumb of some prince, khān or
sheikh, who, along with his family or tribe, was
leading that country on the broad highway to freedom
and development. My mind went back to those days when
I was at this same level in school and we were drawing maps. I saw just how lucky we had been, we children
of twenty or thirty years ago. For the maps we used to
draw, we'd only needed two or three colors for all
of Asia, Africa and Australia. We used to use brown
for the English to cover half of all Asia and Africa,
pink for the French in the other half of the world,
and green, or I can't remember, maybe it was blue,
for Holland and the others. Now...wow! How the children's
work has increased! I said this last sentence outloud,
causing the *nāẓem* to ask, "How's that, *Āqā*?" "Nothing,"
I replied. I asked him what they'd been using the
auditorium for up till now. Obviously for nothing.
No films, no assemblies, no plays. It's only function
was at examination time. If you sharpened your
olfactory nerve just a bit, you could smell the stale
sweat the children poured out during the written
examinations, and sense the heat of their fevers. It
was just like one of those closed rooms where they'd
shut off the stove the day before. I involuntarily
touched the wall. It wasn't warm. 'What pillars they
are,' I thought, 'and how thick and heavy. My, how
well they bear the weight of learning on their
shoulders.' Next, I went upstairs, which houses five
classrooms in a row, with a porch in front, stretch-
ing from end to end and facing the sunlight. The
words of the Koran, in resonant, sonorous tones and

heavily accented stress, rolled imperiously out of the fourth grade window. The sun shown brightly on the barren ground which stretched around the school. The brightness of the individual gables on the roof added even further lustre to the scene. The cry of the Moslems. How wonderfully assuring for the local citizenry who hadn't yet come to lay foundations and dig wells in this ground. Not a single error. Not a solitary hint of this being an inopportune religious entailment. Not any indication of an improper merger. I was sure this teacher was a complete good-for-nothing. He undoubtedly attended nightly Koran readings. The endowments of our schools usually don't even have this much attractiveness to offer. The minds of this place's future citizenry must really be at ease.

The third grade was located at the foot of the stairs. There was a call to attention and rattling of tables. They were practicing dictation. Their teacher, with those pipestem legs of his, was spinning around like a top, reciting, "Sa'di the dervish is humble." I looked over at one of them who was scrawling "dorwash isombul." I moved on. The fourth grade teacher was resting heavily on his chair. It was a wonder the poor chair could support such a figure. Although he was reading from the Koran, one would never have guessed it. If I had gone in, everybody would certainly have leapt to their feet. This prospect wasn't very pleasing, so I merely poked my head in the door, uttered a "Very good," and moved on. The fifth graders were working on percentages and the blackboard was covered with figures. The teacher paid no attention to me. I passed on. I opened the door of the sixth grade. The door wasn't open a crack before I heard, "You motherless..." The young Brylcreemed fellow turned squarely towards me. The face of one of the kids was as bright as a sugar beet. The effect of the insult still smarted. They were having Persian recitation. The teacher, hands in his pockets and chest pushed out, opened his mouth to complain: "Mr. Principal, they just can't comprehend kindness. They need a bump in the head. Notice how I speak with such sincere..." I cut him off at the "ity." "Of course, you're quite correct. Forgive them for my sake this time. They shouldn't be bad boys." And out I went. Next to the sixth grade was a long, narrow room half the size of the others. The door and one window faced south, like all the other rooms, and there was a big window opening onto the north. This was obviously to be my room for the future. With a desk, a set of shelves, and both of them empty. One couldn't ask for more. Peaceful. Sunny. Out of the way. When I closed the door, the Koran reading was completely shut out as well as the daily ruckus in the courtyard. Even if the teachers should have something to discuss, they'd be too tired to come up all these stairs. I arranged my stuff and went back downstairs.

There was a large shallow pool in the middle of the courtyard. It was the only part of the building plan that took children of all sizes and ages into consideration. A volleyball net up at the far end had torn loose in two or three places and was held up by a wire. A high wall surrounded the courtyard, just like the Great Wall of China--a high barrier to meet education's probable attempt at escape. At the back of the courtyard was the outhouse with the janitor's quarters beside it, a storeroom for coal, and then a classroom, the first grade--where the teacher was getting back his abc's from a student up at the blackboard. I went over to inspect the outhouse. As I went in, two steps took me down, then a hallway ran up to a wall at the end. On the left were five toilets. All were roofless and doorless with a partition between each one. The pits at the bottom were visible, and so large that even a cow could sink in. Water was puddled up around the mouth of each hole and signs of the children's fright of falling into such black pits were splattered in all directions. I looked over at the nāẓem who had followed me in. "It's become a big headache," he said. "So far we've written the Building Department hundreds of letters. They say the government's money mustn't be spent on someone else's property."

"They're telling the truth, too," I replied. "The Office of Education's property can't possibly be in such a state of contamination."

We laughed. That was enough. We went back outside. As we came out into the courtyard to catch a breath of fresh air, I inquired about the school's budget and general financial situation. Each room cost fifteen *rials* per week for cleaning, sweeping, burlap and chalk. They considered the auditorium equal to two rooms which made a grand total of eleven. The Office of Education supplied writing and office materials. They also had twenty-five *tomans* per month for drinking water which hadn't yet been collected. Last year's stoves had burned wood, but this year they had to burn coal. The installation charge for each was three *tomans* yearly. The school was also provided thirty *tomans* monthly for miscellaneous items, which, like the money for the water, had been written off as a bad debt. It was now the second month of the school year, the middle of November. I made it clear to the nāzem that I didn't feel like doing this sort of work and summarized for him briefly my reasons for becoming a principal. I told him I was prepared to place full authority in his hands. "Just imagine that a principal hasn't come yet." He could keep the stamp with the school's official seal. Of course I didn't really know him yet. But, in the end, I did have to have a nāzem, and who was better than he? He had run the school without a principal for two months prior to my arrival and had graduated from normal school. He knew what teaching and education were all about and was familiar with all the rest of that malarky. I'd heard that principals are supposed to pick their own nāzem beforehand but I didn't know anybody else. And besides, I didn't have the patience to go looking for another. I had obtained my position only after tremendous difficulties. We finished our conversation and walked back to the office. We drank tea which the janitor had prepared until the bell rang. It rang again and again. I took a look at the students' records, each of which consisted of two sheets of paper--copies of their identity cards, vaccination certificates, and all the details of last year's report cards. That was it. And from these same sheets I learned that the legal guardians of most of the children were illiterate farmers, gardeners, and irrigators. Before the last bell had rung and the school day completed, I left. It had been an awful lot for the first day.

3 The next morning I went to school bright and early. The lines of children were moving off towards the classrooms. The nāẓem, stick in hand, was standing on the porch, and only two of the teachers were present in the office. Obviously, this was their daily custom. I sent the nāẓem off to take care of one of the classes and went outside to pace up and down in front of the school gate. There were footpaths on the north and east sides. Real footpaths--long and straight, running diagonally through the middle of the barren space up to the main street, the asphalted one, where the bus ran up and down. It had trees, shops, and other signs of life. I figured that regardless of the direction from which they'd come, they were bound to see me standing by the school gate way down here at the end. They'd feel embarrassed the entire length of the path and would never be late for school again. I was pondering whether or not it was proper to show such strictness from the very beginning... when suddenly a black shadow appeared at the end of the southern route. It was the kid with the Brylcreemed hair. I recognized him by his short stature and from the way he walked. Certainly he must have been able to see me too. Yet on he came, far slower than a teacher should who was showing up late right before

) 50 (

his principal's eyes. When he got closer, I could hear
that he was even whistling. It was one of those European dance tunes. Undoubtedly, he had to be able to see
me from this distance. I could even see the big
anchor on his tie, battening it down so it wouldn't
shake. I thought to myself, 'He probably owns only
this one tie.' But the ingrate kept coming with such
a swaggering strut that I realized there was no
possible way for me to simply let the matter drop.
He didn't pay me the heed he'd pay a dog. I was just
about to blow my top, when I sensed a change in his
movements. He began to hurry. Buttoning up his coat,
he fixed his eyes on me. He seemed to nod his head.
'Well,' I thought to myself, 'this time it turned out
okay. But, if it hadn't, God only knows what might
have happened! The least I'd have done would have
been to go to my office and close the door behind me,
so that when he came in he wouldn't see me'...After
saying hello, he seemed about to say something when I
anticipated him. "Please Āqā, please. The children
are waiting."

It had really turned out fortunately. He hadn't
seen me for sure. Perhaps he'd been thinking about...
hmmm...I don't know...maybe about some girls he'd seen
last night in English class. He was human, wasn't he?
Probably he had debts to pay, troubles and worries
eating at his heart. After all, a youth with
Brylcreemed hair and an anchor fastened to his chest
could be alone, couldn't he? Perhaps his bus had
been late. Perhaps the road had been closed. Maybe
the street had been cordoned off for a big VIP who
had come from some far off land to enjoy the local
amenities and assure himself a share of free food from
Emām 'Ali. In any case, in my heart, I forgave him. I
was thinking what a lucky break that I hadn't started
railing, when, from a great distance away, the exalted
figure of the fourth grade teacher appeared. He had
seen me from way down at the end and almost broke
into a run. His legs were long. He could run well if
he had to. But his body was heavy. How he was

torturing himself! I couldn't stand this fellow. "You'r[e] not handling this properly," I told myself. "First utte[r] a *besmellāh* and then pick him apart." I went into the office, sat down, and busied myself with something until he arrived, panting and gasping for breath. Such a sweat was pouring from his forehead that, honestly, I felt embarrassed. Even his hello dripped with sweat. I helloed back, wanting to add, "If you hadn't seen me, would you have run like that?" But I felt that that would be mean of me, and changed my mind. I offered him a chair, stuck a glass of water from the pitcher into his hand, and watched his laugh metamorphize in the water as he gulped it down. When he got up to go, I said, "Well, after all that, you're two kilos thinner!" He turned, gave me a glance and a little laugh, and left. I was about to go off to my own room to see whether or not the janitor had straightened it up, when the *nāzem* came pounding down the stairs. In just one day, I'd learned to recognize the sound of his feet. Before he reached me, he exclaimed, "Did you see that, *Āqā?* That's the way they come to school. That first pretty boy could care less, *Āqā*. But this last one..." I wanted to repeat my wisecrack about losing weight, but I realized it was a rather corny joke, and decided against it. "I guess that still leaves two classes free."

"Yes *Āqā*, the third grade has physical education. I told them to sit down and practice their handwriting, *Āqā*. The arithmetic teacher for the fifth and sixth grade hasn't shown up yet, *Āqā*." Then he pulled one of the desks over to the wall, climbed up on top, and pushed aside one of the large pictures of the crypts of the Achaemenids, which had been fastened to the wall. "Take a look, *Āqā*..."

Hurriedly and awkwardly scrawled on the plaster, in red pencil and in not too large a hand, was the sign of the hammer and sickle. Before I could ask anything, he continued, "One of the leftovers from their tenure, *Āqā*. When I came here at the beginning of the year, their principal was still here, *Āqā*. This was the kind of stuff they did. Selling newspapers, spreading propaganda, and drawing the hammer and sickle, $\bar{A}q\bar{a}$. When they were arrested, what agony I went through, $\bar{A}q\bar{a}$, trying to convince them to stop this stuff, $\bar{A}q\bar{a}$. The parents of the children came over here hundreds of times to complain. Three times they came over from the Military Governor to find out where the others were..." He jumped down from the table. The crypts with all their designs at top and bottom, swung back and forth two or three times, and then covered over the sign of the hammer sickle again.

"You mean there are still some left?" I asked.

"That's right, $\bar{A}q\bar{a}$. What do you think I'm talking about? That very gentleman who hasn't shown up yet is one of them, $\bar{A}q\bar{a}$. Everyday he's half an hour to three-quarters of an hour late, $\bar{A}q\bar{a}$. The third grade teacher is another. Whatever you try to tell him, it will be a waste of time, $\bar{A}q\bar{a}$."

"Well, why didn't you clean up this mess before?"

"Wha...Why, $\bar{A}q\bar{a}$, who's a person to tell his troubles to? Why, $\bar{A}q\bar{a}$, right to your face they'd start calling you a spy, an agent. Twice already I've had it out with this one who's late, $\bar{A}q\bar{a}$. It ended in fisticuffs."

He went into a lecture about how they'd ruined the school, how they'd destroyed the confidence of the local people who didn't have any kind of organized council and no help whatsoever for their lack of finances; and how everyday there were problems with the Military Governor...and how they'd turned the children into stubborn unruly jackasses, etc., etc. When he'd finished his lecture, I took out my handkerchief, gave it to him, and he climbed up and rubbed off the sign.

I explained to him that he and I were not *Nakir* or *Monkar*, and that because of the tenor of the times, there wasn't a thing we could do. The Department of Security paid out good money for this sort of thing. There were plenty of experienced agents who knew what they were doing, and there was absolutely no need for him to get involved. We'd be better off

simple minding our own business. Then I headed off
towards my own room. On the stairs it came to me that
undoubtedly in every part of the world they cover over
signs like that with the same type pictures. I opened
the door to my room and was clearing my nose of the
smell of damp earth when the last teacher showed up.
I came out onto the porch, and shouted for the nāẓem
in a loud voice so that everyone in the school would
be sure to hear, "Mark him an hour late in red ink."

4 Again, on the third day, I showed up for
school bright and early. I hadn't yet turned the
corner in back of the wall when the anguished cries
of the children greeted me. I speeded up. Five of
the kids were huddled on the porch while the nāẓem,
stick in hand, whacked them one by one on their palms.
Very official and very proper. Two whacks on both
hands for each of them, and then over again. The
lines of all six grades provided an audience for this
contest. The children were pleading and wailing. But
they stuck their hands out anyway. They were accustomed to it. A couple larger kids were faking cries of
pain. One of them kept snapping his hand downward,
vacating the space immediately below the switch with
such dexterity that I really enjoyed watching. This
big one was undoubtedly the very one who had provoked
the nāẓem in the first place. One of them was so tiny
I doubted whether the switch could even hit his hand.
Aiming at such a hand was impossible; and, for sure,
the birch was going to land on his fingertips. Ouch!
...I knew how much that stung. Or else on the wrist...
I was about to shout at the nāẓem or kick him and push
him out of the way. His back was to me and he couldn't
see me. But as I entered the school, something shining
in the children's eyes startled me; and the murmur
that arose among the rows of kids suddenly dispelled
me of that notion. It is no easy thing for a principal to strike his nāẓem, especially in front of all

the students. With this realization, I swallowed my
anger and walked calmly up the stairs. And just when
the *nāzem* noticed me and his hello was on his lips,
I stepped in and begged him to spare all of them this
time for my sake. I have no idea what they had done:
come late for school, or forgot to cut their hair,
or had dirt in their ears, or didn't have a white
collar, or stole their friend's pencil, or cut up a
seat on the local bus with a razor, or found something
in the street and refused to hand it over to the
nāzem or a hundred other misdeeds. Which is to say
that afterwards the *nāzem* gave me a full report and
also described in detail how badly they usually behaved.
But that little boy's hand had been so tiny, his face
so much like a cat's; and he had shed such tears that
honestly I'd come within an inch of smashing the *nāzem*
in the mouth and breaking his switch into little
pieces over his head.

The children returned to their lines choking and
sobbing. Then the bell rang and the lines moved toward
the classrooms; behind them the teachers, who were
all on time today. After the room had emptied, I
suddenly noticed another switch under one of the
shelves. I cast a glance at the *nāzem* who had just
regained his composure and said, "When you're in
that kind of mood you're liable to break one of their
necks." He bristled. "If just one day you neglect to
keep them in line, they'll climb all over you, *Āqā*."

Like a school boy, he addressed me as *Āqā* in every
sentence. I sensed that if I mentioned one more word
to him about the children, he might oppose me to my
face. So I changed the subject, and asked him how his
mother was. The smile on his face evaporated. He
called in the janitor to bring a glass of water. I
don't know why, but all of a sudden I took it into
my head to counsel him like an old man would. I
related that in all my years in elementary school,
night school, high school and every other kind of
school, I had been punished only twice. When I was
in the third grade, they had given me the bastinado in

front of the whole school. My offense had been climbing to the top of the Mc'ayyer Mosque minaret which towered above our school and had such a spectacular view. The second time occurred in my fifth year of high school, when the school principal grabbed me by mistake and gave me a couple belts. Afterwards, when he discovered he'd gotten the wrong boy, he summoned me to his office and, since I was "one of the offspring of the Prophet," apologized and awarded me a book, which I still have to this day...I recall speaking to the *nāẓem* for over half an hour, just as an old man would. He was young and malleable. After our conversation, I asked him to break the switches, which he did, whereupon I went off to my room.

5

In that very first week, I became familiar with my job. Winter was just around the corner. We had nine coal-burning stoves, four daily deliveries of water, cleaning and sweeping of all the rooms, and with only one janitor, this situation obviously couldn't continue. I petitioned the Office of Education for another janitor and sat in wait for his arrival.

I didn't go to school in the afternoons. I had survived those first few days with fluttering heart and shaking hands. But after three or four days I had found my courage. I sensed that my presence wasn't what was keeping the school running and that if I weren't there, it wouldn't have made a bit of difference. I also knew that in the afternoons most of the classes had physical education. The first grade ran straight through, so I needn't have any apprehension about the littlest ones. Also, the school volleyball net was harmless. And not a single automobile frequented the barren land surrounding the school. Although the land had a lot of irregular dips and rises and was full of flood-caused erosion holes, it was, at any rate,

bigger than the school's courtyard. The teachers took
turns in the afternoons. Two came to school everyday.
They had some sort of arrangement among themselves.
There was no further fear that the kids would get
constipated from too much knowledge! If there
were any danger on that account, it would have been
on those mornings when I was at school.

One day a Ministry inspector came out. We buttered
each other up and shared tea and respectful phrases. In
his inspection book, he certified that the school
"despite a lack of equipment" was being run extremely
well. I arranged for a Public Health doctor I knew,
who still couldn't hide his Qazvin accent under his
scientific and medical jargon, to come out once a
month to check for trachoma symptoms in the eyes of the
children, a duty he performed with such unskilled relish
that he'd nearly blinded several of them. He rolled
back their upper eyelids so roughly and with such speed
that if he'd tried the same on me, I'd have clobbered
him. He noted that we should get some mercurochrome,
some cotton and a roll of gauze from the Office of
Education (which of course had none). With no other
recourse, we were forced to ask one of the children,
whose father was a Public Health doctor in the Army,
to bring the stuff to school free of charge. Arms
or legs were banged up three times a day at the very
minimum. The kids ran and fell down. They went up and
down stairs and fell down. They played, then fell down—
just as if they'd been fed rabid dog poison. More
than anything else, they quarrelled and fell down.
Their simplest game during the fifteen minute recesses
was fighting. All of a sudden, you saw or heard two
of them piling into each other in a corner of the
courtyard. Then one fell down and the fight was over.
Of course, that is, if shouts from the *nāzem* or one
of the passing teachers hadn't put a stop to it sooner.
I thought that maybe the reason for all this falling
down was that most of them didn't have good quality
shoes. Those who did were all mama's boys who didn't
know how to run or in some cases even walk. This

was what caused two or three scraped hands and feet per day, as well as bruised heads and faces, and the office floor spotted with permanent red splotches of dried mercurochrome. The mercurochrome was within arm's reach. They'd come up themselves, rub some on their scrape or cut, and leave. Usually, the older ones helped the younger ones with the *nāzem* or the janitor occasionally pitching in. Even I once bandaged the ankle of that little boy with the tiny hands and the face like a cat's.

The electricity and telephone records I pulled out from the school's measly little file and read through them. If one hustled a bit, in two or three years, both the school's electricity and its telephone might possibly be fixed. Twice I paid a visit to the Buildings Commission and hashed over the matter, and with a few casual acquaintances in the Telephone and Electric Office. Once or twice I put such pressure on them that, for a while, they thought I was trying to use the name of the school in order to swing some sort of private deal for myself. Finally, I had to drop it. This was to the extent I had to go in order to discharge my duties.

The school had no water. No drinking water and no running water. With stagnant water left over from the spring rains, they filled up the cistern under the pool which had a pump they used to fill up both the pool and the kids. During the fifteen minute recess periods, in addition to the yelling and screaming, the wheezing and groaning of the pump filled the air. Actually, the pump was a toy for the children who went wild over the sound of it. Raising a ruckus was another of their little games. They shouted. They shrieked; their shouts and shrieks containing more insults and obscenities than laughter or mirth.

We had two 100-litre containers for drinking water made from galvanized iron. Like twin *emāmzādeh* shrines or twin fountains, they stood on a four-legged stool in the corner of the courtyard. Twice daily they were filled and emptied. As soon as the bell rang, the children swarmed for the water. What a thirst they had--a hundred times greater for water than for learning. We brought the water over from the same garden where the pines rose up, staining the sky with long dark spots. Of course, it was the janitor who brought it. It was good water. At least so it seemed from the appearance of the qanāt. I had checked it out myself.

Whenever we wanted the janitor, he wasn't around. His wife would run out to say that, instead, so and so had gone for water. We fetched water with a big bucket and a watering can with a hole in it, which, by the time it got back to school, would be half empty. I paid for repairs on both the watering can and the pump out of my own pocket. One couldn't sit around waiting to collect the school's petty cash and endure the continual groaning of the pump while the children went thirsty.

One day, the owner of the school came by--an old man, solemn and serious, who thought he had come to inspect his tenant's home. Before he entered the courtyard gate his shouts filled the air, cursing the janitor and the Office of Education for allowing the children to blacken the walls with charcoal. I recognized him immediately from his ranting. We exchanged the usual amenities, turning over bushels of names in search of a mutual friend. It wasn't easy. He was twice my age. But finally we hit common ground and were thus able to relax. From that point we knew what to talk about. Next came his recommendations for the slant roof over the outhouse, which was surely going to leak, and for the outhouse, which was certainly full by now, and for the cistern, which was doubtlessly covered with slime, and for the water pipes lest, with winter just around the corner, they freeze up and crack, and how the Office of Education had sold him a bill of goods and how, if he were in Europe, they'd have made him a member of the Academy by now for his open-hearted generosity. On and on with such inanities and pretensions...We gave him some tea; and he became acquainted with the teachers; and I kept on making promises until finally he left. A real pestering tick. An old washed-up man. The incarnation of bygone memories and meaningless stories about the past—a perfect example of the gravity only advanced age can give a man. He had sat for exactly one hour and a half. This turned out to be a regular monthly performance, which we had to anticipate and be prepared for.

The teachers—that was another matter. Each had an official order saying that he was to teach twenty-four hours per week. But, none were actually teaching more than twenty. The nāẓem himself had set this arrangement up before my arrival. After we gradually became acquainted, we made an agreement that I would request another teacher from the Office of Education and give everyone eighteen hours of teaching on the condition that the school not be closed for a single afternoon. Even the one who attended the university could handle eighteen hours per week. This had been my first difficult hurdle and I had solved it by applying village arbitration techniques. I put through a request to the Office of Education for another teacher.

6 The new janitor arrived at the end of the second week. He was a slender, active man of about fifty with a knit skull cap and a navy blue suit of the same material they use for police uniforms. He rolled a set of worry beads in his hands and was a jack of all trades.

From then on, the janitors took turns bringing water, one one day, the other the next. The school, now spic and span, took on a new lustre. They scrubbed the porches. They also set up the stoves, those same old wood-burning ones and, for their installation, paid out thirty *tomans*, which the nāẓem collected from the Office of Education a week after I signed

five copies of receipts. The two of them together
could easily have taken care of the installation. But
the new janitor had his eye on the money. I overheard
that he had asked, "What about the funds set aside for
installation?" This forced the *nāzem* to hire someone
for the job, who, after his arrival, twirled around
school for two whole days like a *Ḥājji Firuz* minstrel
on New Year's Eve. Before waxing the stoves, he got
wax all over his own face--a bogeyman come to life in
the midst of the kids. Perhaps this was what caused
them to lose all their fear. The two janitors and the
workman changed the three legs of the stoves, covered
over their stands with mud and brick, and put them in
working order. That done, we had to hustle after coal
and kindling. I sent the old janitor to the Office of
Education at noon four days in a row. And we sat in wait
for the arrival of the coal.

Less than a week after the day of the new janitor's
arrival, a grumbling arose among the teachers. The
new janitor not only refused to say hello to a single
one of them, but also wouldn't carry out even their
slightest commands. He didn't pay them the heed he'd
pay a dog. Every morning at eight sharp, like everyone else, he showed up for work. And, although he
hadn't an ounce of schooling, he signed the attendance
book. He scrawled a few lines in front of his name
which, with recourse to geomancy and the aid of an
astrolobe, one could make out to be Ḥosayn. When
the noon bell rang, like everyone else, he would head
for home and in the afternoons do the same. Of course,
he greeted me. But then, all of the teachers surely
had qualities, titles, and credentials equal to
mine, and, in any case, had enough status to expect
a school janitor to say at least hello to them. And
would you believe it--he considered himself on equal
footing with all of them. How he insisted on signing
that attendance book. But worst of all, he was a constant nuisance to the teachers. I had tried from the
very beginning to set myself apart from them, giving
them a free rein so that during recesses they could

go to the office, close the door, relax, and say or do whatever they wished. But now, just as the teachers headed for the office during class breaks, the new janitor would show up. He poured tea for them or gave them water and then remained standing in a corner of the room. The teachers were inhibited by this. With him present, they could never set aside their scholastic manner and for ten brief minutes be themselves. None of them had the courage to let him know how they felt or the cleverness to figure out a way to get rid of him. Once or twice, they sent him after a left-handed monkey wrench. But he was clever and would finish the job in a flash and return. He had become their shadow. So much so that for several days the sound of guffaws and laughter no longer came out of the teachers' room. A storm was surely in the offing. If in all my ten years of experience I had learned one thing, it was that if teachers can't relax and joke during the fifteen minute recesses, they'll certainly take it out on the children during the class hour, and that if they can't relieve themselves of the burden of teaching through the exchange of wisecracks, surely they will consequently fall asleep in the classroom.

 I found myself obliged finally to intervene.
 One day I summoned the new janitor to my office. I began by inquiring about his health and welfare, how many years of experience he had, how many children, how much money he was making, etc...when suddenly the matter resolved itself. Right, he was making over 300 *tomans* per month. Of course, considering his twenty-five years of experience, 300 *tomans* wasn't much. But in a school where the most experienced teacher is making 190 *tomans!*...This was the fly in the ointment. It was obvious now that the teachers had a right to consider him an outsider. He possessed neither diploma nor rank, not even a torn piece of paper; whatever might be said, he was no more than a janitor. And a browbeater at that, albeit with some justification. So, first with hints and allusions, and finally very

frankly, I explained to him that although teachers have no earthly reward, nevertheless, because he was such a religious and understanding man, since he was surely familiar with the expression, "He who has taught me a letter of the alphabet, etc..." He interrupted me:

> "Eh, *Āqā!* What are you saying? You're neither up to this job, nor do you know what kind of people they are. Today they want me to buy cigarettes. Tomorrow they'll send me after vodka. I know their kind. You're just a stranger who happened to drop by these parts. But I've spent a lifetime with these affected phonies."

He was right. He had sized me up quicker than anyone else. He had understood from the beginning that I was a nothing at the school. Now I was afraid this thing was going to go too far and I'd lose face. A school principal remaining silent in front of an impudent janitor..."Vroom, Vroom." I was rescued by the coal truck. As the driver put on the brakes and the sound of the motor died, I said:

> "What you've said is shameful. Where are public school teachers ever going to get the money to buy vodka? Get moving now. They've bought the coal."

And as he was leaving, I added, "A couple days from now, when they need you and come asking for a loan, you'll all become friends." And I went out onto the porch.

They had opened up the school's big iron gate and the truck had come in. They were in the process of emptying the load in front of the storeroom at the far end of the courtyard. The driver of the truck handed the *nāzem* a piece of paper which he glanced at, then pointed to me standing on the porch, and motioned for him to go up. With a hello, the latter handed over the paper. It was the coal bill, the official Office of Education receipt in triplicate, with a typed statement from the weighing station attached stating that altogether the load came to 3600 kilos. But the official receipts from the Office of Education had no figure written in. The place showing the amount of coal delivered to school had been left open on all three copies. Obviously, the receiver was supposed to fill them in. I did just that. I took the sheets into my office, wrote in the figure on every copy, signed them all, and gave them back to the driver. As he left, I called down to the nāzem:

"If it requires the school seal, friend, you stamp it," and went back to work.

I was busy thinking about the new janitor, about his quick mind and his practical experience, about how wonderful it would be if only two of the teachers possessed all his experience and years of service and how, if all of us in our jobs were veterans like him, why the children would be philosophers in one year's time...when the door to my office opened and the nāzem walked in, the coal bill in hand. "You mean to say you didn't understand, Āqā..." "I hadn't understood. But even if I had, it wouldn't have mattered. Because of my untimely stupidity, I lost my temper and asked angrily, "So?"

"Nothing, Āqā...That's just the way they operate, Āqā. If you don't make a deal, they'll mess up our work, Āqā..."

I blew up. Here, with perfect candor, he was inviting me, the school principal, to participate in an undercover deal. "Incredible," I yelled. "And now is Your Excellency going to tell me what to do?...Damn this Office of Education and its principal, me! Go give them back their receipt. Curse on their graves, those bastards..."

I gave out a shout no one in the school could possibly have expected of me. I had been an acquiescent and accommodating principal, who always politely requested and never ordered anyone and one who escorted every grocer and illiterate farmer to the door because I knew that the children's parents had an even greater need to learn these courtesies then did their kids. And now here was the school's nāzem teaching me how to accept, say, 5400 kilos of coal instead of 2700 so that afterwards I could strike a bargain with the Office of Education.

Until noon, I couldn't do anything but write out the text of my letter of resignation, rip it up and begin again...This is how they take the first step against a man.

7

When the rains began, I ordered the stoves lit each morning from seven o'clock on. According to regulations, we weren't supposed to begin using them until the second week in December and then only after eight o'clock. But we started ten days early. Coal or wood, we used whatever was available. Each afternoon we prepared the stoves for the following day. The children's old exercise sheets were always in abundance, so all that was needed was a match.

The kids always came early. Even on the rainy days. They must have been thrown out of the house at the crack of dawn and got no lunch before the afternoon session. I have no idea what it was at school that made them come with such enthusiasm. Whatever it was, it certainly wasn't education. Certainly it wasn't for love of their lessons. And certainly not for the sake of their teachers, their nāzem, nor their principal, who coldly acknowledged their hellos. I tried hard to just one day make it to school first. But try as I might, in the end, I never did succeed in inhaling fresh school air free from the "contaminated-with-learning" breaths of the children. Sometimes my work carried through the noon hour and I didn't leave for lunch until one o'clock. Yet even at that time, the school was so crowded you'd have thought it time for afternoon classes to begin. They always came early.

And as soon as they arrived, they gathered around the stoves and dried their *givehs*. A number of them even stayed at school through the lunch hour. I quickly discovered that their staying through the noon hour was caused by a shoe problem. Whoever had shoes didn't stay. This rule also held true for the teachers who stayed behind in order to keep at least one day ahead in shoeshine money.

Rain that falls in a mountainous area isn't just a one or two hour affair, and both foot paths running from the asphalt street to the school were dirt. The constant traffic of passing children had turned them into narrow paths resembling those worn by sheep on the way from the fold to the stream; paths which are permanent quagmires, filled with mud, stagnant water, and sewage. The school's courtyard was even worse. Playing and running had been suspended and the school became lifeless as a grave. No one had forbidden a thing. Here again, the problem was shoes.

Before experiencing all of this, I had read reams of nonsense about the basic elements of child training and education--about certain fundamentals like having a good teacher, clean toilets, blackboards, erasers, and a thousand other things...But here, very simply, the fundamental and primary element was shoes and shoes alone. *Givehs* become heavy in water and if you go too fast they stick in the mud and your feet come right out of them.

Besides showing up for school in wet clothes and with hands turned beet-red by the cold, the majority arrived with eyes red and puffy. It was obvious that by the time they got to school, they'd already cried rivers of tears, and that in their homes, learning was their sole road to salvation. The fathers of most of them were either illiterate farmers or gardeners --undoubtedly prolific progenitors all, and hence overburdened with offspring. My interest in all this didn't spring from pity or any sense of altruism. The point was, our school was slowly ceasing to function. The number of absences in the morning was now ten times what it normally was; during the first hour not one teacher could hold class. Swollen, frost-bitten hands cannot function. The *nāẓem* had broken his switch ages ago. Even the first grade teacher comprehended that learning in our schools depended totally on one thing and one thing alone. Practice. Drill and practice. Ten times and twenty times over and over and over. Yet, if frozen, frost-bitten hands cannot even use crude instruments like shovels or planes which fill up the whole hand, how can they possibly be expected to manipulate pencils?

This started me thinking.

The new janitor was sharper than any of us. One day we held a sort of council meeting in the office and naturally enough he was present. Proving himself fully able to take complete advantage of the teachers' youthfulness and stupidity, he had little by little imposed himself on the group. Now, in this session, he offered a plan. He was prepared, he said, to persuade one of the school's well-heeled neighbors to send over some sand for our courtyard on the condition that we agree to present a request to the town council for clothes and shoes for the children. The third grade teacher exploded from his chair like a firecracker. "Are you proposing that we act like beggars? It's beneath the school's dignity. Cottoning up to assemblies like this inspires evil suggestions ..." If our council had been ripe for it, he'd surely have gone on to recite all that he had memorized about the postponing of the Communist Revolution. But the council wasn't ripe and, as a result, I wasn't forced to intervene. I accepted the proposal.

Until that time none of us, neither myself nor anyone else, had heard a word about a town council. We decided the janitor should pursue the matter himself, find out where next week's council meeting would be held, and, if he wished, procure some kind of invitation for us.

Two days later three trucks pulled up filled with sand. We emptied two of them in courtyard and dumped the third in front of the school gate. The children themselves flattened out the sand in a half hour's time, using their feet, shovels, planks and whatever they could get their hands on. The father of one of the children had sent it over. Naturally, we lined all the children up and made them give a rousing cheer in hopes that our patron's life might be long and auspicious. That afternoon, the fellow himself showed up and invited us to such and such a house, on such and such a day, at such and such a time, so that we might become acquainted with the council members.

Naturally, the *nāẓem* and I were obliged to go. We also decided to take along the fourth grade teacher, even though I feared they might mistakenly consider him to be the principal. He was a most appropriate addition. He spoke pompously and was indeed the pride of teachers everywhere.

The house where the meeting was to be held stood alone in the middle of nowhere, like an out-of-the-way school house. Each of its walls seemed to spring directly from the heart of the desert. The sun had already fled by the time we arrived. The house had a huge iron gate which we passed through, entering into an orchard full of trees yellowing with the autumn season. There were two sandy paths leading up to the house, which resembled a big European hat set down in the middle of the yard. Numerous servants were hanging about. We gave them our hats and raincoats as we passed through the entrance. They led us into a hallway, up a staircase, past some bronzed-over, plaster statues, each one with a light on its head. The muffled chugging of a generator under our feet and through the walls followed us in. They obviously had their own electricity. We soiled their lush carpets and hall rugs with "education" and marched on. It seemed to me as if they'd thrown them down three deep so that after the first got dirty, they could switch to the second. Upstairs we came to a large salon. We entered. A *Ḥājji Āqā* dressed in old fashioned, loose, white under-trousers with a very wide crotch was in the midst of his prayers. Just as he brought his head back from the prostrate position and I was able to catch a glimpse of his beard, the owner of the house came forward, welcoming us in his thick Yazd accent. As I introduced my companions, our host caught on immediately which of us was the principal.

All of the lights were twinkling, making the sight of our opulent surroundings a bit easier to endure for us who had come from the educational realm. Tea was brought, very weak, and served in delicate cups with enamelled silver handles. I couldn't get down even half of mine. I lit a cigarette and commenced a conversation with the owner of the house about his carpets. He was a rug merchant. The more a rug is trampled the greater its export value. Our conversation was moving from there to the export market, when Hājji Āqā descended from his throne. He rose to his feet, pulled on his trousers, rearranged his genitals, mumbled an old fashioned greeting in Arabic, and made some welcoming gestures in similar style. The fourth grade teacher kept right with him, meeting greeting with greeting, compliment with compliment until soon they were engaged in spirited conversation. The nāzem, on the other hand, looked like one of those little children who get sleepy at adult gatherings, but refuse to go to bed.

The members of the Council began arriving one after the other. From the way in which each paid his respects and exchanged compliments, it was possible to figure out who was who and who did what. Hājji Āqā was the treasurer. I remembered seeing the name of the one who was head of the Council in the headlines of newspapers from I don't know how many years back. He had been expecting a ministerial appointment then. Now, he was basking in the "Yes, sirs" of the members of the local Town Council and managing the town's water, power, and garbage disposal problems. He must have puffed with pride at the thought of the directors of the local school humbly coming to solicit the benefits of his good counsel. "Wouldn't it be wonderful," I thought to myself, "if all the ministers would be content to open their ministries on the street corners in their own districts like him." Tall and short, young and old, in all fifteen people had arrived.

We got up and sat down over and over again as each one entered. The *nāzem* and I were behaving just like the two children of *Muslim ibn 'Aqīl* while the fourth grade teacher sat between us like *Khuli*. The members of the Council surrounded us, each leaning comfortably on his property, his wealth, and his summer home. The majority spoke with provincial accents and behaved like country bumpkins. Not a one knew his ass from his elbow. They blew their noses noisily and stared at us. You'd have thought this was the "Ministry of the Beasts of Burden" and that three new animals had just been admitted to the local zoo. One of the younger ones, who wore glasses, looked just like a monkey who, by wearing glasses, was imitating a human being.

The meeting was called to order. The owner of the house introduced us, and they commenced. First, approval of the minutes of the last meeting, followed by a listing of the absentees. An exact copy of a National Assembly meeting. They were taking it all so seriously that occasionally I forgot where I was. First off, they discussed the robbery which had taken place the night before last at *Āqā* so-and-so's home, resulting in his absence at tonight's session. All agreed they would now certainly be forced to request another police station or, at the very minimum, a night patrol. Next, on to the dried-up wells, the electrical plant several companies were supposed to build, and the deep well the owner of the house wanted to dig.

The next point of discussion concerned the problems created by so-and-so renting his house out to an American. When the rental came to an end, without any expense or effort whatsoever on the landlord's part, water, electrical and telephone facilities had been installed right up to the edge of the bed. An envious murmur rumbled through the assembly. Ḥājji Āqā begged everyone's forgiveness, and...This is the way things went for a solid hour as matters of high import were thoroughly dealt with, discussed and investigated. Ḥājji Āqā played with his worry beads. The one with glasses kept pretending to be a human being and the forth grade teacher and I smoked cigarettes. It was as if we weren't even present. When the servent came in to collect the tea cups, I wrote a note on the back of my package of cigarettes, and gave it to him to pass to the owner of the house. Suddenly, our host remembered us. He requested the permission of the assembly, and began: "These gentlemen have a petition. It's better for us to take care of the other affairs later."

This was his way of making it clear that it wasn't wise for them to discuss all these other issues in front of us. Permission was granted and the fourth grade teacher began:

"Yes. In accordance with an expression of willingness by you gentlemen yourselves, we have come here in your service..."

The gist of it all was: "Whatever you decide, we remain under the protective shadow of you auspicious gentlemen, who should certainly confirm that it isn't proper for gentlemen's children to have classmates with neither hats nor shoes and that we were informed of your philanthropic nature and wished to take this opportunity to express our thanks for the truck loads of sand." It was beautiful. Elaborately delivered with exactly the right emphasis, just like a Director General. He knew why we had brought him along. Next the nāẓem, freshly startled from his doze, began reciting the phrases he had memorized. Beseeching and pleading, he did everything but recite a prayer from the Koran. He ruined everything. He was just about to make the rounds for a collection and, by virtue of putting everyone on the spot, cause them to dig into their pockets, when I completely blew my stack.

I snapped at the *nāẓem* to stop his bloody begging, that it should be patently clear to the group that this wasn't a supplication for charity, and that we were not freeloaders. On the contrary, the school was located in an out-of-the-way place, the Office of Education was preoccupied with its own problems, the toilets were in a state of neglect...and much more such nonsense...What good fortune that I hadn't gotten angry. The one who was imitating a human by wearing classes had come to my aid. Whenever I was about to lose my temper, I'd glance over at him. I spoke for a good quarter of an hour. It was decided that tomorrow afternoon, five of them would visit the school for an inspection tour. They would take care of anything outside the responsibility of the Office of Education. With expressions of gratitude, appreciation, and what a pleasure it had been, out we came.

Outside, in the darkness, seven cars were lined up, one behind the other, in back of the house wall. All the drivers had piled into one car and were busy divulging the secrets of their masters' harems. We set off on foot towards the street where the bus ran. I offered the fourth grade teacher another cigarette so that I might use the match light to search his face for a sign of something I thought might be there. But it wasn't. I couldn't find what I was searching for. In the session which had just ended, not only had they removed his teaching mask from his face, but they'd also lifted completely the grandiose air from his Director General's stature. Nothing of his real self remained. Does that mean that I too had that same expression on my face? That very same expressionlessness? That same face full of emptiness? Yes.

Why had I ever gone? Because the children were without shoes and hats? What's that to me? You'd think I were to blame for their shoelessness and their hatlessness. How did I get mixed up with these beggars? "Now do you see, stupid? You became a school principal and you've got to wrap up your personal dignity and pride in tin foil and stow them inside your hat so that they don't rot. Or else, sew them into a green cloth to hang around your neck, so as to at least save yourself from the evil eye. Even if you were just a mere unimportant teacher...No, why make a far out analogy? Even if you were a 90 *toman*-a-month janitor, you would still have to sink into slime up to your Adam's apple. You wouldn't be any better off. Public servant! Damn the whole business! Isn't that the way it is?"

We walked on, side-stepping the piles of brick, lime, and cement which lay in our path. The vanguard of the honorable citizens of the future. I don't know whether I sighed, said something, or what. But, in any case, both of them turned my way. The *nāzem* said, "Did you see the way they treated us, *Āqā*? He could buy up the whole school, *Āqā*, with just one of those rugs." The *nāzem* was trying to make amends for his sermonizing.

"As long as your job is teaching abc's," I replied, "be careful of the deductions you make. You'll end up eating your heart out." The fourth grade teacher spoke up: "Even if they'd cussed us out, I'd still be satisfied. One's got to be realistic. God will it they don't regret their decision."

We commiserated with one another at the bus stop, until the bus arrived and we got on. I learned that the fourth grade teacher was recently estranged from his wife and that the mother of the *nāzem* had been diagnosed cancerous. Finally, we bid each other good night, and went home...

I didn't go to school for two days. I was too embarrassed to look either of them in the face. In those same two days, *Ḥājji Āqā* and three others arrived to inspect the school and draw up a list of our needs. The *nāzem* told me that even the children who had decent clothes had come to school in ragged condition. Eighty sets of clothes. I excused the new janitor and ten of the children from the last class hour every afternoon from the fourth day on,

)73(

so that they could go down to the bazaar shop of Hajji Āqā. From that day on, the number of children with only one galosh mysteriously increased. The tailor took down their measurements and arranged for all the clothes to be ready ten days later. During t[] course of the following days, I had the feeling that the women who habitually washed their dishes in the stream running along the footpath on the way to school were saying hello to me. Once, behind my back, I heard one of them give a prayer for my healt[] I was so disgusted and angry with myself that I derived no pleasure from looking at all the new shoes and clothes. Blessed be those same ripped *givehs*. The beggar's bread had bedecked education in a new suit of clothes.

8

I had just gotten over the initial headaches of running the school when one morning, one of the parents showed up. "Greetings. How are you?" We shook hands. He sat down, stuck his hand into his inside coat pocket, took out six pictures, and put them on my desk. Six pictures of naked women. Stark naked. Each one in a different suggestive pose and in each pose, a thousand lewd suggestions. 'Hey, what does this mean?' I gave him a hard look. He was a neatly dressed, proper-looking individual. An office employee, most likely, or maybe a real estate man. Although I had seen pictures like this a few times before in my life, never had I wished to offend the illusory world of my imagination with such made-to-order prints, prints which every impotent fool carries around in his pocket as a kind of aphrodisiacal auxiliary verb. I considered it a detraction from my personal dignity to observe this particular aspect of life in accordance with the orders of the head photographer of some port city

whorehouse. I'd always considered them with the same
eye that looked at a butcher's meat hook--as something
to hang food for thought on. Yet now, here before me,
was a neatly dressed man in freshly ironed clothes,
preparing to smoke a cigarette while waiting for the
utter immodesty of these pictures to fill my eyes. I
was completely astonished. I had never considered
that as a school principal I'd get involved in these
kinds of problems. I was totally taken by surprise.
Even on that day when the skinny little policeman
came to school to complain about his son, and, on dis-
covering we had broken the switch, took off his own
belt, wrapped it around his son's feet, laid him out,
and urged the *nāẓem* to whip him ten times on the
soles of the feet with a ruler--even on that day, I
hadn't been surprised. After all, he'd had policeman
written all over his face, and had his own particular
reasons for his approach to life. "Why then did God
create the whip?" he'd argued. He'd recognized the
tools of his trade to be among the necessities of
creation even to that extent. But, this fellow? Who
was he and where had he come from?...A full minute
went by before I looked at all six of the pictures.
They were all of one girl. I avoided an immediate
confrontation by allowing myself to escape into vis-
ions of thousands or even millions of these pictures
existing at this very moment in other people's
pockets. What kind of people were they and where in
the world were they located? Wouldn't it be wonderful
if I were acquainted with all of them, or at least
had a chance to see them? Smoke from the fellow's
cigarette filled my nostrils, bringing me back to
reality. Avoiding the issue any further would be impossible. This man, with every ounce of shamelessness,
was sitting right here in front of me. I lit a cigarette and looked him straight in the eye. He looked
harassed. Obviously he'd come prepared to fight.
His face had reddened and he was searching in the
smoke of his cigarette for some refuge from which he
might summon the boldness he'd hoped to display.

) 75 (

I covered the pictures over with a sheet of paper blackened by doodlings I'd scribbled earlier in the day. Then, in a tone usually associated with the opening to an argument, I asked: "Okay. What's your point?"

My voice reverberated around the room. It was obvious that if I hadn't spoken firmly, he'd have saddled up his charger and lit into me. He squirmed about helplessly, and put aside his challenging demeanor. In a manner far softer than that which he'd brought with him into the room, he replied: "What can I say?...Ask your fifth grade teacher."

I breathed a sigh of relief.

He continued, "What kind of an educational system is this? The devil take it! Oh, Islam. What confidence can children have in this school?"

And on and on with more of the same...Some of what he said was true, some of it false.

To summarize, the fifth grade handicrafts teacher had given these pictures to the gentleman's son with instructions to paste them on plywood, sand the board down with emory paper, and return it to him. The rest was perfectly clear. Either this fellow was one of those obsessive fathers who inspect every minute detail of their child's life and, hence, through constant pestering, quickly drive the child into open rebellion, or else his child was one of those spoiled brats who never take a drink of water without first asking their parents' permission. It didn't make any difference. Whichever the case, the fifth grade teacher had leapt before he'd looked. And now what was I to do? How could I answer this man? Should I tell him I'd fire the teacher--which I neither had the power to do nor saw the necessity for? What could the poor teacher do? Obviously he didn't have a friend or relative in the whole town. He was obliged to content himself with such pictures. But why oh why did he do it this way? Was he that stupid that he didn't even know his own students? Did he have to pick this particular kid to give his pictures to?...I got up to call the nāẓem. He had already come up on the porch and was standing outside waiting. This was the way it always was. Whenever anything happened at school, I was always the last person to find out about it. If they were able to handle things themselves, either for better or worse, I'd never even be informed. If something they did got to me, it was proof that somewhere along the line they'd been stymied. He entered. The presence of this parent had left me befuddled--that such pictures should be in his son's pocket. Why, he undoubtedly must have taken them from him with the very same shamelessness he'd displayed in throwing them on my table! When the fellow realized that both of us were quite overpowered by the situation, he seized the initiative and lit in. He vowed he'd do this and do that, close down the school, demand the interpellation of the Minister of Education, and a hundred more nonsensical threats...Obviously, he didn't realize that if the door of every school were closed, the door of every office would also close. He was unwittingly taking the bread right out of his own mouth. Again, he spoke about the Moslem way of life, about the position of the teacher and the words of the Prophet urging us to study from cradle to grave, and on and on with more weighty topics. As long as he was there, I was unable to gather my wits. He wanted us to call in his son to testify and be cross-examined. What a battle we had convincing him that his son had suffered enough humiliation. We made promises to skewer and roast the teacher in the noon-day sun and fire him on the spot. The nāẓem began by claiming how he too had a score to settle with this teacher. I picked it up, continuing about how we had no choice but to kick him out of school. When the man finally left, we two were left sitting there, alone, with six pictures of a naked woman, whose nudity was now veiled by my doodlings.

When I regained my composure, I instructed the nāẓem not to breathe a word of this to anyone. I kept the pictures and the story behind them locked safely in my desk drawer for one whole week. Then, I called for the boy. He was neither one of those spoiled brats, nor was he any other particular type. He still had another three or four years to go before reaching puberty, had a very pale face, and was small for his age. His shoulders reached only two finger breadths above my desk. He was obviously from a very large family. Anemic and underfed I realized that his teacher hadn't done such a bad assessment job after all, which is to say that he hadn't really leapt without looking.

"Do you have any brothers or sisters?" I asked.
"Ā...Āqā, I do, Āqā."
"How many?"
"Ā...Āqā, four, Āqā."
"Was it you yourself who showed these pictures to your daddy?"
"No, honest Āqā...Honest to God."
"Then, what did happen?"

He was fairly dead from fright. Even though the nāẓem had broken the switches, his fear of me, the principal, of the nāẓem, of the school, and of the punishment which was surely to come had remained completely intact--particularly in regards to the nāẓem. I saw that I'd have to put him at ease.

"Don't be afraid, sonny. This has got nothing to do with you. It was the teacher's fault who gave you those pictures...You didn't do anything wrong, sonny. Do you understand? I just want to know how these pictures got to your daddy."

"W...W...Well, Āqā...Well..."

Clearly, if he were going to talk, I was going to have to help him. I didn't enjoy playing spy or holding mock trials--especially with a child with no color in his cheeks. I didn't want this affair to force me to extract information from him. But of course all these thoughts were impossible to explain to him. The nāẓem had appointed one of the kids monitor. I knew who the boy was. If, at the beginning, I'd turned all of this over to him, we would have been free of it on the very first day. Now I had no choice but to continue. I asked: "Do you know, sonny? These pictures aren't anything bad. Did you yourself understand what they were?"

"Well, Āqā...No, Āqā...My sister, Āqā...My sister said..."

"Is your sister younger than you?"

"No, Āqā. She's older, Āqā. She said that...She said that...Nothing. We argued over the pictures."

That finished it. He had shown the pictures to his sister who kept her notebooks crammed with pictures of movie stars and singers. He had tried to lord it over her with his pictures, and hadn't been willing to give her even one of them. Should a child whom the teacher trusts make such a mistake? How could he answer to the teacher now? Clearly his sister had betrayed him. She'd gone and tattled to their father, a man who up until then had had no desire whatsoever to keep constant vigil over his children's comings and goings. The father had found the pictures and the beatings had followed. Now at last both of us were freed.

Later on, I summoned the teacher to my office. He knew immediately the reason for the summons. Obviously, there was nothing he wished to add. After a week of grace, he was still in a state of amazement that I, who had discovered his complete shamelessness, had desisted from picking on an unarmed man. To tell you the truth, I was a little embarrassed. But there was really no other choice. I had to smooth this thing over somehow. First, I put his mind to rest regarding the little boy who was actually quite blameless. Then I told him to sit down, offered him a cigarette and told him this story. One day during the early days of the Ministry of Education, the Minister was informed that such and such a teacher was having an illicit relationship with such and such a little boy. The Minister immediately summoned the teacher to his office. After asking him about his life and how he was, the Minister inquired why, up until then, the teacher hadn't taken a wife. As it turned out, the problem was money. The Minister ordered that the teacher be given enough money to allow him to marry and the Minister himself was invited to the wedding. He had solved the case just that simply. I went on to add that today there were also many young men who couldn't get married. But nowadays the Ministers of Education were so busy giving radio and newspaper interviews, attending receptions and giving parties that they didn't have time to attend to such matters. But, nonetheless, the doors of plenty of good families were still open...I continued with this kind of nonsense...and sympathized and commiserated and didn't let him get in a single word edgewise.

Finally, I took the pictures out of their envelope, stuck them in his hand, and, by saying this final sentence, raised to the ninth degree the utter immodesty and shamelessness of this whole affair: "If you don't paste them on a board, they'll cause you less trouble."

9 It took three months for them to transfer my name to the local Office of Education's salary list. And how happy I could afford to be at this delay. It so happened that the accountant of the Office of Education had chosen this very same time to up and flee with the salaries of all the teachers, all the janitors, and all the principals, along with the salary of the Chief of Education and all the special post and family allowances of this district' "government ration-eaters"--the impoverished educationalists, beggar-hungry, down to the bare bones, and with hands longer than their feet from being constantly stretched out, palm upward. It was rumored that he'd gotten away with fifty to sixty thousand *tomans*. I am positive that during those days, huge numbers of homes in the area under the Office of

Education's jurisdiction had their morning tea cut off. Fortunately, from our standpoint, we had a rich janitor who could loan everybody money. Little by little, he'd become the school's bank. Out of his monthly wage of three hundred some odd *tomans*, he didn't spend more than fifty. He didn't smoke, he didn't go to movies, and he had no other expenses. In addition to all this, he was also a gardener for one of the school's well-heeled neighbors. He had a garden all his own, which was quite a spread in its own right, with all necessities provided, including, no doubt, a beautiful kitchen. This fellow didn't roll a set of worry beads for nothing...His reverence for money had long since bridged the gap between him and the teachers. I didn't make any inquiries but it was obvious he wasn't collecting any interest from them. Thus, our teachers didn't have such a bad time of it. They quickly realized that a rich janitor is much more useful than a principal with nothing to offer save his title. So much for the teachers. My salary was still being paid out of the Central Office. As for the others in town, they were undoubtedly adjusting to the delay in similar ways. Or so I gathered, since nothing had changed and the waters remained calm. The thief had up and vanished from the face of the earth. Yet, twenty-five days later, when the investigations began and a second money order arrived from the Ministry of Finance, classes were still operating as usual. Orders were still being signed. The office typists were still pounding away from morning till noon, and the office record books continued to blacken. The only observable difference was that now, whenever you saw the Chief of Education, he was always in a sweat, having "just this minute" come back from Tehran, where he had "done such and such in the Central Treasury Office" and "personally spoken with the Minister."

My name was transferred to the Office of Education's list starting with the next month's paycheck. For that first month, I wrote up my own time card, affixed my own signature, and went off to my old school where I formerly taught, to pick up my salary. Becoming a principal at least had this advantage. Now, with my own signature, I could introduce myself to the cashier's office where the paymasters were noted for being as strict as Allāh's prophets. One must be a "government ration-eater" to appreciate the value of this privilege. Perhaps this was the real reason why schools never remain long without principals, or other big cheeses to watch over everyone's shoulders. There was this to consider too. The accountant at that school wasn't very bright and by the time he realized my timecard was approved by my own signature he'd already handed over my money. However slowly the wheels of office red tape might revolve, they were faster than the thought processes of that school's accountant!

Whenever the hue and cry of salary arose, the teachers snapped to, and for three or four days out of the month, the entire school functioned at full capacity, that is, until I signed the timecards. Save for that one time early in the school year when I'd put down a red mark in the attendance book for the fifth and sixth grade arithmetic teacher, I'd never used the red pencil again. Hence, the minds of all were at ease. Nonetheless, their salary allotments were still dependent on a single signature. And, even though their salaries would certainly never fall into arrears when that signature was in the hands of a principal like me, even then, don't forget, I was a human being like everyone else. There was always the possibility that I might take a disliking to one of them, and then what? The teachers certainly took this possibility into full consideration, because every month, two or three days before timecards were to be signed, they always shaped up.

When I went down to pick up my own salary, the Office was so crowded I wished my name had never been transferred. It was noon time. Every man and woman was struggling to climb up on the head and shoulders

of the one in front of them. It looked like a bread
shop during wartime. If you said to hell with it and
tried to leave, there was no way you could get out.
For those in front of the cashier's counter, any
show of magnanimity, self-respect, or the slightest
hesitation was a crime punishable by branding irons.
After all, wasn't the "government salary-taker"
nothing but an open bag in front of the paymaster's
counter?...If you tried to wait in that crowd, you'd
be standing till two in the afternoon. I kept smoking
cigarettes and walking up and down, waiting for the
tumult to subside. Time and again I acknowledged the
greetings of this one coming and that one going. All
of the "office ration-eaters" had gotten wind that I
was a principal and they were practical enough to think
that maybe one day they'd end up teaching at my
school. I learned that day for the first time that
one out of every three had already spent half of his
monthly salary, or had received an advance, or purchased a carpet or a samovar on installments or had a
promissory note to be deducted. The former accountant
had rifled the kitty and now all of the accountants
were hopelessly interlaced. Grief and pain is the
short and narrow path. They chased after promissory
notes, they cussed out the former accountant, they
begged their creditors to forget this month's payments.
All of them suddenly became lawyers and arithmeticians.
When one received his money before his turn, all
howled in protest. The observance of manners on that
day so upset me that I prepared myself for a two or
three day delay before picking up my own salary. The
worst of it all, however, was yet to come. The largest
figure of all on the school's salary list belonged to
me. It stood out like the biggest sin at Judgment Day.
I was making twice as much as our new janitor. When
I saw the moribund figures of the others' salaries,
I was so ashamed one would have thought that I personally had stolen their money. For two whole hours
I walked up and down, giving all of them full
priority over myself and wondering whether or not I

should pay some kind of atonement. Never once in thos[e]
two hours did I stop to think that not one of them
had even a third of my experience nor half of the
torn bits of paper which I had long since rolled up,
stuffed into some back closet of my life, and forgott[en].
This is the kind of philosophizing I do these days fo[r]
my own edification. But, on that day, all I could fee[l]
was that when others were receiving wages this meagre
and this insignificant, how could I, even though I
was but another unknown "government rationeater" myse[lf],
how could I hold myself blameless? This thought tor-
mented me. Finally, when the room emptied and after
I had signed in ten or fifteen different places, the
cashier glanced up at me, and, with a thousand
apologies, pressed six hundred *tomans* of "stolen
money" into my palm...The s.o.b!

10

One afternoon, when the first snow was
still on the ground, the fourth grade teacher was
hit by a car. Run over by a private automobile. Like
all afternoons, I wasn't at school. It was sunset by
the time the school's old janitor brought the news to
my house. I leapt for my clothes. While I was getting
ready, I could hear him describing to my wife what
had happened. That afternoon, the fourth grade teache[r]
had left school (just like every other day) and was
walking home with another teacher, when a car ran hi[m]
down. The car belonged to one of the Americans who ha[d]
recently moved into town in order to bring water and
electricity along with him to the area. The servant
told me the rest when we got outside. It seems the
fellow himself had been behind the wheel and that
after the accident he'd been so stricken with fear t[hat]
he'd up and fled. The children had brought the news
back to school. But, by the time the janitor and his
wife got to the scene, the people and the policemen
had already picked the fourth grade teacher up and se[nt]

him to the hospital. From the looks of the blood which they'd cordoned off with stones on the pavement, his corpse was all that had made it to the hospital... When I got up to the bus, I saw that it was moving no faster than a turtle. I dismissed the janitor and jumped into a cab.

I headed first for the new police station which had recently been opened at the request of the town council. Brand new and right in the school's backyard. "Greetings!"

The guard on duty was that same policeman who had visited our school and personally administered the bastinado to his son. After exchanging greetings, he pieced together what had happened for me. He had access to the case's full file. But the file didn't specify who the driver was. All the data was in order—the report of the patrolman at the scene of the accident, finger prints, and the number of the station's record book. But no one knew what had finally become of the fourth grade teacher. All that the guard knew was that in this type case, "in accordance with administrative procedures," one must first go to the main police station, then to the traffic accident center, and then to the hospital. If we hadn't been acquainted, the guard on duty would never have allowed me to get so much as a furtive glance at the case file. I sensed that I had, little by little, become a well-known figure among the local residents. This sensation gave me a chuckle. I hopped back into the cab and took off, following those same "administrative procedures."

Finally, at eight o'clock, I arrived at the hospital entrance. Even if the fourth grade teacher had been healthy, if he'd carried out these "administrative procedures" from four-thirty in the afternoon until this time of night, something had to have happened to him, just as it had happened to me. The door to the hospital was huge. It gave off the smell of a mortuary. On it was written, "No Admittance after seven o'clock." I knocked. Someone yelled back this same message from behind the door. I knew immediately it was hopeless. If I were to get in at all, I'd have to summon help from another source. A show of force, a flaunting of title, physical strength, something. I deepened my voice and yelled back, "I'm..." I was about to say "the school principal," but regretted this idea immediately. He would only have answered, "The school principal? Which dog is he?" The doorman of such an imposing door, whoever he was, was no little Corporal pulling guard duty at a newly-built police station, who could be counted on to accommodate the local school principal. Thus, after a slight pause, with a voice full of authority and officialness, I finished my sentence, "...inspector from the Ministry of Education." The wooden bolt clunked and the door opened a crack. I adjusted the expression on my face to match the sound of my voice. The door opened a little wider. The fellow on the other side nodded a welcome and pulled his grey-smocked form away from the door. That was all I saw of him. I went in, and, in the same voice, asked: "This school teacher who was in the accident..."

He understood and before I could finish my sentence had already called someone, sending him trailing after me with instructions to go to such and such a floor, room such and such. In the midst of the darkness outside, five or six lone pines stood out against the sky. But no smell of pitch came from any of them. All that was in the air was the faint smell of camphor. I set such a pace that the fellow following behind was panting. From the courtyard to the corridor, and again, on through another courtyard. I don't know whether my companion was thin or fat. What I mean to say is that I didn't bother to look. But panting he was, and hard. What exquisite pleasure I took in forcing one of those phlegmatic philosophical "that's life" types into running. First floor, second floor, fourth floor. Four stairs at a time. The hallway was dark and filled with all kinds of weird smells. The wall clock had stopped at quarter past eight. Clack,

clack, clack. The nails in the bottoms of my shoes echoed up and down the brick floor of the corridor. I'd assumed all of the tough demeanor of a police official on his way to make an arrest. I was prepared to slug the first person who might appear before me and dare tell me, "No!" I resorted to everything I could think of to increase my anger and sense of outrage. I even forced my thoughts back to that horrible evening with the town council, to all those prayers and supplications, and to the sense of amazement we had created. Others build houses that they might collect their rent money in dollars; the fourth grade teacher in my school gets run over by one of their foreign tenants; and I, at this time of night, need a disguise in order to visit the poor devil. And I could do nothing about any of it. These thoughts passed through my head during those few moments I stood under the stopped clock on the wall. What I am trying to say is that I forced myself to think these thoughts while waiting for my companion to catch up. The darkness inside was blacker and the smell stronger. It was a large ward filled with beds, the squeaking of shoes, and the labored breathing of one of the patients. Four people were circled around one of the beds. This had to be him. When I got to the foot of the bed, all of the anger, affection, and assumed authority which I had summoned to my aid dissolved into sweat and went running down my forehead. I had run all the way. My breath was short and my legs were shaking. And here was my fourth grade teacher. Big-bellied and heavy, he lay stretched out on the bed. His magnificent Director General's frame seemed to have been crushed lengthwise by a press. He looked much smaller to me now than he had when he'd been on his feet. His head and shoulders were outside the death-stained sheet which covered him. There was a swelling the size of a pillow underneath the sheet in the place where his right foot should have been. They had just wiped blood from his face, which was now black and blue, the color of a mark left by a hard slap on a child's face. When he saw me, he broke into a smile, and such a smile it was. Perhaps he was trying to say that a school whose principal is not on the job in the afternoons deserves this fate. But he was unable to speak. They had wrapped his jaw up with a handkerchief, just like a dead man's. But he had a smile on his lips and he wasn't yet on a slab in the mortuary. The smile, which had replaced the blood spots on his face, had frozen, just like water in a pool which, in early winter, first shimmers, then forms wrinkles, and finally freezes solid. The smile quivered, shook and quivered in just that way until finally it froze. "Why, oh why, did you have to have an accident?..." I must have asked him that question. But when I saw that he couldn't speak and that instead of a response all that appeared on his face was that frozen smile, I continued for him: "Why, why? Why did you have to flaunt that great Director General's body everywhere you went until they finally got you, until they ran you down? You mean to say you didn't know that a teacher has no right to cut such a figure? Why did you have to be such an eye-stopper? You used to be even too big for the foot paths. You used to block the thoroughfare. Didn't you know that streets and traffic lights and civilization and pavement all belong to those who, in cars built in their own country, trample the rest of the world? Oh why, oh why did you have to have an accident?"

I spoke these sentences so reprovingly that I am not at all sure now that I didn't actually say all of them to him outloud. Suddenly the thought crossed my mind, 'You idiot, curses be upon you. After thirty odd years of life, you now become superstitious?'
I was so disgusted and fed up with myself I wanted to cuss somebody out, to strike out against someone. My eyes fell on the doctor.

"The devil take this whole country. Do you realize this man has been bleeding since four-thirty this afternoon? Don't you have any pity...?" A hand dropped onto my shoulder, suppressing my shouting. I

) 88 (

turned around. It was his father, with that same
Director General's body, and that same face. His son
was indeed a chip off the old block. But, now, the old
block was only half the size of the chip, darker and
more withered. Every whisker in the old man's white
beard looked like it had been planted one by one into
his sunburnt face. He too was smiling. He held his hat
in his hand, uncertain where he should put it. Two
other people were with him. All three were village
types, broad shouldered and tall in stature. What a
pleasure to see. How strapping and healthy they were,
all of them. The other two were either sons, nephews,
or relatives. I was beginning to cheer up when I
heard: "Who are you, $\bar{A}q\bar{a}$?"

It was that same doctor on duty. Again I leapt to
the attack. "Do you mean me, $\bar{A}q\bar{a}$? Me? I'm a nobody.
Just some insignificant school principal. And this is
my teacher. A morsel for your dissection room..." At
once my reason urged, "Shut up, boy!" And at once I
shut up. A lump formed in my throat. I wanted so badly
to get in just one more lick, one more sarcastic
remark, one more snide smile, to take just the littlest
of nips...I hadn't found a doctor yet whose abilities
I would swear by. I'm certain this fellow knew at least
a smattering of psychology. He stepped forward friendli-
ly, offered his hand, and I reluctantly shook it. He
then pointed to a large bottle hung upside down over
the bed and demonstrated for me in a manner that even
a fool could understand that this was the way they
fed him, that they had taken x-rays, and that tomorrow,
provided his wounds hadn't become infected, they were
going to set his broken bones in a plaster cast. At
that moment, another arrived, stethoscope in hand,
white smocked, and perfumed. His mannerisms resembled
those of the popular movie stars. When he said hello
to me, the sound of his voice shook a small compart-
ment somewhere in the dusty corners of my brain. But
there was no need for further inquisitiveness for he
was one of my former students from God knows how
many years back. He introduced himself. "Why, Doctor
...How the time flies!"

My mind drifted: 'You earned your daily bread by putting every ounce of your energy, along with all the nonsense you could muster, into sowing seeds for the future. Now witness the fruits of your labor. You have eyes, idiot!? Do you see a single trace of your influence on this man? Look at the marks of the movie industry on his forehead? You were carried away by your illusions. You flattered yourself. Okay. Suppose you had been right. Tell me, now, after ten years, do you still have seeds left to sow? To scatter? Huh? Don't you think that now you are just like this flattened out carcass? All you have left is the trace of a bitter smile painted across your face. You've fallen to a point where now you're under the subjugation of yesterday's children. Is that you who is stretched out on this bed? For ten full years, with every passing moment, the minutes and the hours of your life have ticked away and moved up the staircase of life. All you have to show for it is the weariness of the load lingering in your body. This strutting bantam rooster and all the other young cocks whom you don't know were hatched from eggs you once nurtured, eggs which have long since been cracked open and left empty. And now, wherever you look, not a single trace remains, not a cracked shell or even a feather...And what about this one on the bed? He didn't even have a reprieve from this. Before he could make something out of his miserable profession to take some pride in, he is crushed and ground under by the wheels of civilization. With that magnificent physical presence. And that speaking ability which was the pride of the entire school...'

I took the doctor's hand, led him aside, and whisper in his ear every single swear word and insult that I could think of, against him, his colleague, and his whole profession. Did you think that I was going to beg him to please take special care of my fourth grade teacher? Then I nodded to the father and fled.

When I got outside, I found myself in a courtyard. The weather had turned rainy. I walked along slowly, attempting to deposit with the dampness of the night all that lingered in my nostrils of medicine, pain and regret. I tried to keep myself from becoming emotional. When I went out into the street through the big front gate, I thought to myself, 'What is any of this to you, really? Why did you come at all? What could you possibly do? Did you have to satisfy your curiosity? Or play at being a humanitarian? Or pretend that you are a conscientious principal by posing as an official inspector?' I finally concluded that bait for the fat-tailed officialdom of the police department and the justice department had been procured; and not only was I not going to be able to get that bait away from them, but there was nothing else I could do either. As I was getting into a cab to take me home, the thought suddenly struck me: 'You should have at least asked what happened to him.' I wanted to turn about and go back. But that big, swollen, black and blue body of the fourth grade teacher was there, stretched out on the bed, and I realized that I just couldn't do it. I was either too ashamed or too afraid. Of him, or of that bantam rooster hatched from an egg. Or of his father or of the smiles which all of them had on their faces. 'Why oh why hadn't I been at school?'

I stayed awake that night until two A.M. and the day afterwards wrote up a long report signed by me, the principal, with all the teachers as witnesses. I submitted it to the Office of Education and the local police station. Then I rushed down to the Insurance Office to arrange for nine *tomans* a day payment towards the hospital expenses. In the afternoon, after waiting a bit, I went to school, cancelled all classes, and sent the teachers and the sixth grade students to visit him. I arranged for flowers and made other attempts to do the right thing...For an hour I walked up and down, alone, in the schoolyard. Free from the hurly-burly of classes, I lost myself in reflections...

The next morning his father showed up. After we exchanged greetings, he said that one arm and one leg had been broken and that there had been some slight internal bleeding in the brain. People on behalf of the American had come to the hospital with promises and commitments to give him a job with Point Four, just as soon as he was well again. The father made it clear to me without coming out and directly saying so, that I had submitted my report rashly and to no good purpose. But, now that I'd already gone ahead and submitted it, I shouldn't follow it up. Both sides were fully satisfied, and I was being "more Catholic than the Pope"...Curses on this damn country.

11

I hadn't paid the children much attention at the beginning. I thought that the difference in our ages was so great it would be better if we had as little to do with each other as possible. I had read reams of b.s. about how the ages of student and teacher should not be too far apart, about the generation gap and the differences between the men of yesterday and the children of tomorrow. This kind of crap... I was busy with my own work. I closed the door to my office and, in the warmth of the government stove, went about my scribblings with one of those "a hundred for a half-a-*dinār*" pens. But this routine lasted no more than three or four months. I wearied of it and found myself obliged to become more and more involved in the school's affairs. As I did so, I began to uncover all kinds of things I hadn't known about before. Oh, how the old teachers of my schoolboy era were missed. What a crowd they had been. Anonymous, unknown characters, each one with a silver tongue and his own unique set of mannerisms. And now these young dandies- a bunch of harmless camp followers for those Europhile among us who worshipped everything Western. They hadn the foggiest notion where they'd come from, nor the faintest understanding of the new property which, after having seventy different hands in the pie, had

) 92 (

finally been alloted to them. Their complete total ineptitude was worst of all. For example, it never once occurred to them to one day collude together and bring about a complete halt to the school's daily routine. Not for a week, but just for a day, or even a single hour. Quiet and regular, just like the daily train to the *Shāh 'Abd ol-'Azim* shrine, they quietly came and quietly went. All they knew how to do was show up ten or fifteen minutes late. But their narrow-mindedness was worse even than this. Three times I was a witness to quarrels over a single flower pot. We had a lot of children whose fathers were gardeners and each of them, at a least once a month, brought to school a pot of carnations, chrysanthemums, or a hanging candle holder—gifts which were real blessings in that cold, snowy climate. At first, I planned to use the flowers to decorate the school. But, why bother? There was nobody to take care of them. Who would water them? This was quite legitimate. After all, the children brought the flowers for their teachers. What did the school have to do with flowers? Why, undoubtedly even Plato's Academy had been transformed into an Arabian desert the moment its students first tread on its floors. But worse even than all of the above was the teachers' complete and total lack of personality. It totally overwhelmed me. They couldn't speak two words about anything, not about the world, culture, art, even about the price changes in the bazaar or the cost of meat. They were completely uninformed and ignorant. What an incredible bunch of good-for-nothings. I had the feeling that instead of the students, the teachers were the ones sitting in the classrooms, growing older day by day, and changing from week to week. As a result, I determined to be more attentive to the children.

The kids had dealings with the *nāzem* only. As far as I was concerned, all they seemed to owe me was a half chewed hello. Yet, in spite of all this, they weren't actually discouraging. I began observing them in the foot paths on the way to school. I surprised

them at the corner of the school wall, hoping that f
overhearing a half-finished insult or an uncompleted
sentence I might be able to at least guess at their
inner thoughts and feelings. But, they continued to
run along on their way without even a hello. I was
certain that within a half hour's time, their faces
would be red with tears. It made me sick to look at
their shoes and hats. I determined to be even more
attentive to their behavior patterns and eating habi

Very few of them came to school alone. It was clea
that somewhere along the way they stopped to wait fo
each other. Either that or they gathered in one anot
homes. Drawing near to the Wall of Education undoubt
edly required companions and supporters. Three or fo
of them came with escorts. A servant or a housemaid
trailed along behind, carrying their school bags to
from school. None came by car. Seven or eight had
fathers who owned automobiles. I knew that for a fac
But the road which led up to the school could break
two car springs in a single day.

Of the twenty or thirty that stayed at school
through the lunch hour, only two brought a rice and
meat dish. The school's old janitor kept me abreast
all the news. The rest ate cheap meat patties, chees
and walnuts, stewed dishes, and similar-type stuff.
Two brought only *sangak* break. No handkerchief, no t
cloth, no school bag. They were brothers. They split
the bread between them and stuffed it into their
pockets. Every noon, just like the ones who went hor
for lunch, they set out from school. They had surely
discovered a snug corner in the desert somewhere,
where they could wolf their bread before returning.
I only observed their leaving. Yet each day even
these two bought two or three *rials* worth of junk
from the school's janitor. Licorice sticks, paper
tatoos, pencils, and gum. They bought it from that
same janitor for whom I collected five *tomans* per
month for caretaking services. I had introduced
him to one of the local shopkeepers and set things
up so he could purchase stuff on credit, resell it

) 94 (

the kids, and pay it back in installments. He now considered himself a landlord. Whenever I arrived at school, or whenever I wanted to leave, he ran forward to get my raincoat. Although I pointed out to him everyday that I wasn't used to this kind of red carpet treatment, he continued his obsequious service day after day. In all the time I was principal, never once did I, in his presence, take off or put on my raincoat by myself. What a torture it was. It was just as if someone were sitting in front of me watching me eat and counting each bite I took. There he stood, directly before me, looking me square in the eye. I always asked him about his health and inquired after his wife and children. Before I sat down to begin straightening my desk for the morning, he commenced his reports. Yesterday, two of the teachers had quarrelled again over a flower pot, an official from the Military Governor had come over, the inspector had said such and such to the nāzem, one of the schools had received their petty cash, the head clerk at the Office of Education had been changed... The new janitor clearly had a hand in this. Each morning for a half an hour I was thus forced to serve time at hard labor. I realize now, when I look back, that considering my afternoon absences, this situation wasn't altogether ineffective. One day, while delivering his customary reports, he mentioned that the day before one of the children in the fourth grade had brought two cones of sugar to school and sold them to him. As if I were completely aware of what had transpired, I casually inquired:

"How much did he want?"

"I gave him two *tomans* for them, *Āqā*."

"Say, you really put yourself out. Didn't you ask where he got them?"

"Why should I, *Āqā*? Am I my brother's keeper?"

Way back when I first arrived, he'd never been so expressive, nor so flippant. The new janitor clearly had a hand in this newly discovered ability at repartee. 'Everybody in this school is learning something save me and the children,' I thought.

"Why didn't you speak to the *nāzem*?"

) 95 (

I was aware that he and the new janitor considered the *nāzem* a rival wife competing with them for my favor. Subsequently, they hid many things from his view. These two, like all the other "government ration eaters" of the Office of Education, were well aware that the *nāzem* controlled the school's expenditures. They were undoubtedly figuring that if I took this responsibility over, there might be something in it for them. Hence, their unjust discrimination between the *nāzem* and myself. The janitor was uncertain how to respond to my question. The door opened and the new janitor walked in:

"If he'd told him, *Āqā*, he'd have had to give him a cut..."

I scowled and replied:

"Look, Pop, are you still getting into everyone's hair? Haven't you learned yet that you don't go walking into people's rooms without first knocking?"

I asked them what the boy's name was, convinced them it really wasn't very important, and sent them out to bring me tea. Then I rushed to finish my work and hustled down to the office. First I asked the *nāzem* how his mother was feeling, and then commenced thumbing through the children's records. I quickly discovered that the boy in question was a repeater and that his father was a merchant in the bazaar. Then I returned to my own room and wrote a note for the father, requesting him to come to school the day after tomorrow. I gave the note to the new janitor with instructions to deliver it and bring me back a signed receipt. Two mornings later the father appear One must be a school principal to understand the responsiveness parents show towards the tiniest, mos insignificant order issued by their children's schoo I am convinced that if you sent an official from the Registry of Deeds after them, they would never hop to like this.

He was a man of about forty-five, with an old fashioned, buttoned-up collar, no necktie, and a lon overcoat which resembled the robes mullahs wear. He embarrassed. He hadn't even sat down before I fired out: "Do you have two wives, $\bar{A}q\bar{a}$?"

I had made predictions to myself about this boy and had decided to circumvent the father with this approach. If my question hit the mark, fine. If not, it could be easily remedied. My intuition had been correct because he clearly wasn't shocked by my question. It sounds amazing but a school principal can become as familiar with a man as the public bathhouse scrubber. The fellow probably thought his son had divulged it. I ordered tea for him and offered him a cigarette. He awkwardly puffed away out of a fear lest he let himself go and blurt out a "What's it to you, mister? Mind your own business." I allowed him no respite and pursued my original question.

> "Of course you will forgive me. Because this is surely the reason why your boy has remained in the same class for two years. You will have to admit that when a student brings a cone of sugar to school from his father's house, there've got to be reasons..."

I had begun to lecture him. Suddenly, he burst out: "I swear to you, $\bar{A}q\bar{a}$, every day he's got four *rials* in his pocket. That no good, ingrateful..."

I convinced him we weren't talking about pocket money and that I didn't want him to get angry. I made him promise not to mention any of this to the boy and continued my lecture about how his son was surely not receiving the love and affection at home which he should and that he considered himself an outsider in his own home. He didn't feel that what was his father's was his own. If today he brought a cone of sugar to school, next year he might try to open a sidewalk rug business. I gave the man all kinds of divinations and more nonsense. Finally he shed his bashfulness, opened the door to his heart, and unbosomed all his troubles; about what a bitch his first wife had been, and how his son by her had taken

) 97 (

her side, how after the divorce he'd had several children by his second wife, how this young jackass should be taking care of himself now, and how his second wife with two small children of her own had every right not to pay much attention to him...Now that all the cards were on the table, I began another lecture. Suddenly, I came to. What am I doing? Here I am citing God, the Prophet, and the Koran. That was when I stopped.

After he drained the last of his tea, made his promises, and left, I fell to thinking: 'Heaven forbid that the educational theorists hatch eggs with two yolks in just this same fashion.'

12

One morning when I arrived at school the *nāẓem* hadn't yet appeared. This was an event of rare occurrence. Naturally no one had rung the bell. Although ten minutes had elapsed from the time when it should have rung, the teachers were still relaxing comfortably in the office, talking spiritedly and exchanging jokes. Although I too had been infected by this same disease when I was a teacher, it wasn't until I became a principal that I fully realized the exquisite pleasure teachers derive from going to class five minutes, no, only two minutes, or even one minute late. These teachers clung so tenaciously to the habit that you'd have thought they'd become teachers just for the sake of experiencing these one or two minute delays. But they had every right. When a man is forced to make faces which not only nobody laughs at, but which he himself doesn't enjoy making, he clearly must take some action. I ordered the bell rung and the children sent to class. Two of the classes were without teachers; the fourth grade, whose teacher was still in plaster at the hospital, and whose substitute still hadn't coordinated his schedule with ours, and the third grade, whose

slender teacher had been in hiding for a month out of
fear of the Military Governor's office. The fellow
he'd sent as a stand-in hadn't come in that day. I
sent one of the sixth graders to the third grade to
give them dictation and I myself went to cover the
fourth. Even though you're a teacher, you've got to
practice lest you lose your teaching touch. I had
looked over their homework and was in the midst of
teaching Persian reading when the janitor came in to
inform me that a lady was waiting to see me in the
office. I figured it must be that same idle woman who
dropped by school once every week under the pretext of
checking up on her son. She was a short, pale woman
with large sad eyes, blonde hair and a round face.
She didn't look twenty-five; yet her child was in
the fourth grade. The first time I saw her, she had a
thin blue bandanna over her hair and was wearing an
orange dress and lots of makeup. She was "so pleased
to make my acquaintance" and had heard all about my
"grace and learning." She evidently hadn't learned
yet that school principals, if they hadn't actually been
castrated, were an infirm and irritable lot. She had
simply come forward for the opportunity of exchanging
a few words with a couple of men. According to the
nāzem, she'd been divorced for a year now and, all
things considered, her frequent presence around the
school created considerable headaches. A beautiful
woman out here in the middle of nowhere with a school
full of frustrated bachelors...this would never do.
Every time she came, from that first time on, I made
it as difficult for her as possible. But it didn't faze
her a bit. She would ask for the nāzem, head for the
office and wait until the bell rang and the teachers
congregated. Words and smiles would be exchanged.
Then she'd say goodbye and leave. It was all quite
harmless. Every time she came, all I could think of
was how hard-up she must be to be satisfied with talking to school teachers and how void her life must be
of men for her to be eager to inhale air which people
as useless as these teachers breathed. I was most
concerned about her hard-up state. She seemed to fairly
swallow the teachers' breaths with her eyes; and when

she looked at me, I felt she wanted to devour me. Although I didn't want to cause her any undue distress, I wasn't about to allow her to flaunt her childish self-indulgence in my realm or jurisdiction. And, from another standpoint, I didn't at all like the idea of the school becoming a nurturing place for the teachers' character development, and particularly not in this area...And now, probably this same woman had come. Before starting downstairs, I began laying out in my mind all the shocking things I could say to get her out of our hair. I opened the door. Hello...Wow! What a surprise. It wasn't her at all. Instead, I found a twenty-one or twenty-two year old girl with a large mouth and coarse hair, which, with obvious difficulty, she collected in a bun in the back. Whether you agree or not, I could make out faint traces of makeup on her face. All things considered, she wasn't too bad. But it was obvious that she was a school teacher. I introduced myself as the school principal and she handed me her orders. She'd been to normal school and had only recently been hired. They had sent us a teacher. I wanted to say, "Doesn't the Chief of Education realize this place is overly masculine?" But I saw that there was no real need. Here was some variety. After all, she was female and so could lend a touch of feminine elegance to the school's rough and tumble, boyish environment. I welcomed her, ordered tea, which she didn't touch and, since we didn't really have anything more to say, took her to visit the third and fourth graders, making it clear that she could take whichever she preferred. We discussed the possibility of her teaching eighteen hours, which was the load she had in mind. Then we returned to my office. She asked if, in addition to herself, we had another female teacher.

"Unfortunately," I replied, "the road to our school wasn't built for ladies' high-heeled shoes."

She laughed. I sensed her laughter was a trifle forced. She then hemmed and hawed a bit, finally commenting:

"I've heard you are very good to your teachers..." She had an attractive voice. What a pity, I thought, for her to have to ruin this pretty voice at the foot of a blackboard.

"But not enough to make the school close down, madam," I answered. "Certainly you've heard that your colleagues sat down together and decided on eighteen hours a piece. I had nothing to do with it."

"You're being modest."

I didn't understand what she meant by this "You're being modest," but clearly she wasn't talking about class hours. Instantly, I decided to test her.

"You should also keep in mind the fact that only two of our teachers are married."

She blushed, and in order to avoid showing a further reaction, got up and picked up her orders from my desk. She shifted her weight from foot to foot. I realized I was going to have to come to her aid. I asked her what time it was. It was time for the bell. I called to the janitor to ring it and then suggested that perhaps it might be better if she consulted with the Chief of Education once again. In any case, we'd be only too happy to have the honor of working with a lady like herself. Then I bid her good day.

As the bell sounded and she walked out the door, all the teachers rushed up, as if their hair were on fire, to catch a glimpse. Each one stared after her until she disappeared through the school's big iron gate.

13 The following morning it was evident that the nāẓem was having troubles again with his mother. She was supposed to go into the hospital so they could give her radiation treatment for her cancer. From the beginning, I had done all I could for him. I'd asked a couple of my former classmates who had gone on to study medicine to help him out. But after they'd gone ahead and set aside a

) 101 (

bed for her, she'd become frightened and refused to go. The *nāzem* now wanted me to intervene officially. He wanted me to go with him to their home, and, to quote him, use my "silver tongue" to persuade her to go. At least this is the way he put it to me...I had no choice. From his eyes it was obvious that he hadn't slept a wink the night before. With him in this condition, we couldn't keep the school running. So, I entrusted the school to the teachers, and off we went, by bus and by taxi, finally through the long, narrow, back alleyways, until at last we arrived at his home, which was nothing but a sub-let room the size of your palm in the corner of the lessee's courtyard. The width of the pool measured the size of a single footstep. His mother, with eyes dreadfully sunken, was just sitting there when we arrived. Her face looked like she'd rubbed charcoal on it. It wasn't really black, but the color was dark enough to frighten me. You couldn't call it a face anymore. It was nothing but a big black sore which had split open in the places where her eyes and mouth used to be. Talk and more talk about her son and how good he was, his boyhood days, the weight of his present responsibilities, and how today's hospitals just couldn't compare with the hospitals of the old days. More of these lies until finally we threw her *chādor* over her bandanna-covered head.

"One, two, three, *yā 'Ali*..."

Another taxi, another bus ride, and finally the hospital. Until noon we went from room to room examining beds. This wall was too damp. Those sheets should be cleaner. Finally, we succeeded in getting her to sleep. Then we ran into two or three more of my former pupils, exchanged wisecracks, enjoined them to do what they could, and finally, at one o'clock in the afternoon, we were finished.

The next morning, when I got to school, the *nāzem* was in good spirits. Clearly, he was out from under a heavy burden. He informed me that they had caught the third grade teacher, who had been in hiding for a

) 102 (

little more than a month. We'd been giving his time card to his unofficial substitute so they wouldn't cut off his salary. We continued to do this until the word became official and the newspapers printed the story. The case went before the Office of Education; and his name was striken from the salary list. And now that the news was official, they weren't about to send us a "qualified replacement." We should have followed the regulations. This was the worst of it. All of this aside, how in the world, I wondered, could a fellow with his pipestem legs and tottering body possibly survive the stocks and chains of that black pit and come out alive? Why hadn't I spoken with him? Why hadn't I made him realize that it was all useless, that it was futile? Wasn't I really partially responsible? Not once had we chanced to meet on the road to school so that I might have asked him how life was treating him. He had actually shied away from me. I, who had done so much for all of them, including even the janitors. But what difference did it make to me? For the next two or three days I continued to hold myself responsible and remained upset until finally I decided to visit him. Then I worried about leaving the school empty and the children with nothing to do. We still had seen neither hide nor hair of our substitute for the fourth grade teacher and now here was another class which would not be covered. From the beginning of the year, we had been entitled to another teacher, who was supposed to be sent over to take on those hours I had so leniently allowed to be split up among the others. Once again, I determined to pay a visit to the Chief of Education. According to the Chief, I had clearly scared off the girl. "You started wisecracking before she even arrived." This was the way the Chief of Education viewed the situation. According to him, she preferred to work under him as a bookkeeper in his office. Then, promises and more promises, tomorrow and the day after, until finally, after four days of hustling, I picked up my two teachers. One was a pale, young, polite fellow with thick, coarse hair from Rasht. The other was another of those Brylcreemed young gentlemen. This one changed his tie everyday. And such weird designs and patterns. Our other one had only that one tie, the yellow one with the big anchor in the middle, which he wore everyday even though it had long since grown stained and dirty. But this one. You would have thought he were sitting on top of Croesus's fortune—or else his father owned a haberdashery. Everyday a different tie and such patterns. One, a big palm tree extending up to the knot and below the tree a huge lake emptying onto the boy's chest. Another, a bleeding heart with a line of music complete with notes. You could smell his eau de cologne begin to fill the room before he even reached the door. Incredible how the Ministry of Education crawls with these pretty boys. But what will be, will be. With a come-what-may attitude, we stuck him in with the third grade. In any case, he couldn't be any worse than his predecessor. And now that the school had once again settled down for business, I went back to my work.

One day in the middle of February, the nāẓem came int my office and announced that the school's budget had been approved.

"Congratulations. How much did you get?" I asked.

"Nothing yet, Āqā. They're supposed to come here tomorrow afternoon to work out the details."

The following day I didn't even bother to go to school. He was surely hoping I'd be present to supervise the transaction of the fifteen *rial* per month cleaning charge for each room and to outlay some of my own funds stemming from my position as principal, so that we might have a chance to collect the school's petty cash, the water allowance, and the rest of the back money due us...

The next day three men showed up—the head accountant from the Office of Education and two of his flunkie They had lunch at the expense of the nāẓem, complaining all the while about why so and so (me) hadn't come along. Afterwards, they added up their note pads and documentation charges, manipulated the accounts to their satisfaction, and gave them to me. Without so much as a look, let alone a second thought, I scrawled my signature at the bottom of each. They made arrangements for a second luncheon and left. The *nāzem*, without actually saying so, made it clear that the next time I would definitely have to participate. The way he explained it, we should be thankful that, after inspecting us, they hadn't asked for so much as a fig. They'd been quite satisfied with the one luncheon. To be brief, three hundred some odd *tomans* were set aside in the school principal's account as an entertainment allowance to provide for such luncheons. This was the first time in my life I had even been so important. Here indeed was another advantage in being a school principal. I was beginning, little by little, to really understand what goes on in a principal's heart of hearts. Three hundred *tomans* of the government's budget dependent on whether or not I went to such and such a gathering. Three hundred *tomans*, which, for every two *toman* item, twelve *rials* worth of paper, ink, invoices, and notebooks, was expended. Only when a man is in a situation like this can he truly understand the meaning of the words "office" and "ministry."

My mind is a complete blank concerning what I did up until the day of the luncheon three days later. I can't even recall if I went to school or not. If I did go, I can't remember what I did there. During the entire time, I was preoccupied with one thought: 'Should I go or shouldn't I? Should I go or shouldn't I? For God's sake, are you going or aren't you? Now do you see, stupid? This is what they call the first step. This is the way it always begins. First they create a situation like the one in which you are now caught. They sculpt out a personage for you, give you a position, and honor you with importance. They blow you up like a balloon and tie you to the branches of a locust tree with thorns behind every blossom. The situation they prepare for you doesn't allow you to ever figure out what's going on. Exactly like right now. Your school's *nāẓem* is discouraged and upset. Naturally, on account of having a principal like you. And he has a right to be. He doesn't want to be ground under by the system. He doesn't want to remain a *nāẓem* forever. You know. The whole bit. Promotions, excess pay, a principalship. Up and up and up and up. And here you are pussy-footing around. To make matters worse, his mother is completely dependent on him. It costs money, you know. You can't give tips to hospital nurses on one hundred fifty *tomans* a month. You don't know of any other *nāẓem*, do you? And, even if you did, was he a *Salmān* or *Abāzar*? And, honestly, even if you replaced these worthless dandies with *Salmān* or *Abāzar*, tell me now, would it make a bit of difference? Gone is the era when they wouldn't try to light their own homes with money from the school's kitty. You can't remain the house eunuch any longer nor can you do the *nāẓem* job by yourself. Either fish or cut bait. Quit and get out or take the first step. Go ahead, give a luncheon and then later on, eat someone else's. Pay debts, collect I.O.U.'s. Further on, take the second step and then the fourteenth and then... Ah, the Director Generalship and the edge of the abyss. A complete "government ration-eater." Opportunistic, in tune with the times, glib-tongued, fastened like a tick to the regulations, to retirement, marriage allowances, expense accounts, entertainment funds...Eeeee!'

I was suffocating. Once again I stuck my letter of resignation in my pocket and, without a word to anyone, when the day of the party rolled around, I didn't go.

I soon realized this approach was not going to work. 'I should go before the Chief of Education,' I thought to myself, 'and explain my problem.' I went. His office still looked like a bridal suite, with that same desk and that same empty ashtray gleaming up at me. But by this time, the Chief had grown accustomed to the smoky breaths of his principals.

"Good morning. How are you today?"

I sat down. But what could I say? How should I begin? Should I say that since I didn't want to participate in a luncheon, I was submitting my resignation? Wouldn't that be just a bit ridiculous? Or should I explain the problem more frankly? If I did that, mightn't he feel hurt?...I realized there was absolutely nothing I could say. Besides, wasn't it disgraceful to hand in a resignation, up and quit just for the sake of three hundred *tomans*? What was it that happened to the man in the story who put his head in the lion's mouth? I continued this line of nonsensical reasoning a little further. 'No. Stay. Stay on a little longer. When your time comes to have your head crushed and your neck broken, better to get run over by his car than be crushed by his child's cart. It's more respectable...' I laughed at my own thoughts.

"Goodbye. I only dropped by to pay my respects."

A few more lies later, I was free again in the street. As I walked home, I threw my letter of resignation into the gutter.

But there was still the nāzem to think about. He was as ornery as a stray dog. Growling and belligerent, for a whole week. Early morning switchings of red swollen hands started again. You don't really think I had the courage to interfere, do you? I didn't even dare inquire about his mother. For the entire week, each of us was an independent government within the school. When I arrived at school, I stole ever so softly into my office, quietly closed the door behind me, plugged my ears until the supplications of the children died, and paced from one end to the other. What a torture. Why? Why had I come? I didn't know myself. When I thought about it, I realized that in all my life, in every crummy place I'd ever been, I had always slowly sunk deeper and deeper into the muck, until

) 107 (

I finally grew so accustomed to the stink that I lost even the desire to cry out. Surely that slender youth (I'm talking about my third grade teacher), surely he too must have grown inured to the torment and the torture of prison. I had heard about the horrible things they were doing to him.

For ten full days, my heart and the hearts of children beat together in fear and trepidation. Finally, at long last, our budget was issued. The only thing missing was that instead of three hundred and some odd *tomans* for the principal's entertainment allowance, there was only one hundred and fifty. The reason for this was that "some mistakes" had cropped up when they were doing the figuring and they had been forced to correct them.

14

In addition to that woman who dropped by once a week, two or three other parents were also regular customers. One was the policeman who had tied his son's feet with his belt and given him the bastinado. Every now and then he would show up. At each appearance, he clacked his heels together, snapped a salute, and, regardless how we might beg him, remained at attention—even when we asked him to sit down. Another was a Post and Telegraph employee who came by once every ten days. He was the father of the smart aleck who had whipped his hands under the switch with such dexterity. He came for half hour visits and we would sit and commiserate with each other, talk politics, discuss the salary of grade five in the Civil Service pay scale, talk about his three children and his wife who was afflicted with a serious mental disorder one month out of every year, his one hundred forty *toman* monthly rent, and...The other was a master carpenter whose son was in the first grade. The carpenter could read and write and he boasted

grandly about his son. This man looked like he knew
his craft. He had large hands and slender wrists.
He would take my hand in both of his and squeeze.
This was his way of showing devotion and sincerity,
all the while begging me over and over to please
refer any carpentry work to him, so that he might
"prove his devotion by deeds." I reckoned that
wherever he'd gone to school, he surely must have
enjoyed it. Now, he imagined every little 'Ali-Ābād
to be a city. Then there was a tall, thick-boned
well-digger, whose son was in the third grade. He
came over once a week, would stand in the courtyard
exchanging news with the janitors and quietly
leave. He seemed to have no special business, wanted
nothing from us, and had no words of advice to pass
along. The first time he came, at the time I had
no idea why, he climbed on top of the school wall,
and was shouting for help when I arrived. This
was during those days when "the beggar's bread was
bedecking the school in new sets of clothes." From
a distance, I thought it was someone from the telephone company who had come to install a new telephone pole. But when his shouts and shrieks struck
my ear, I speeded up and hustled the rest of the way.
All the children had poured from the classrooms and
the nāzem and two of the teachers were struggling
to get up the edge of the wall to grab his feet and
pull him down. They were probably thinking one
mustn't be allowed to climb over the Wall of Education so easily. All I could think about was how in
the world did he ever manage to get himself up there.
After I discovered he was a well-digger, I wasn't
surprised. What was more surprising was how he
ever managed to stuff his husky physique into narrow
wells and qanāts. Climbing walls was about all a
figure like his was good for. The gist of his
screams and shouts was to protest why we hadn't given
his son's name to the Town Council so he could pick
up a free pair of shoes and a new suit. This was
his main complaint. Arriving on the scene, I shot a

glance up at him, and then shouted to the *nāẓem* and the teachers to release him. The children returned to their classrooms. Then, without looking at the man, I said:

"Don't work too hard, Capt'n."

Heading for the office, I looked over at the *nāẓem* and the teachers and added:

"I can see you didn't give this poor devil much of an answer, driving him up the wall like that. When a man's got a question at school, you take him to the office."

A whomp sounded behind me. I walked through the door of the office and he and the *nāẓem* came in together, behind me. Instead of being that sturdy figure on top of the wall, he was a stooped man with curvatures in three places, his knees, his waist, and the nape of his neck; and in his whole lifetime, he obviously had never spoken with a school principal. When I told him to have a seat, he seemed to crumple into the chair, and, instead of saying something or responding to my questions, he burst into tears. Incredible. Really loud. "Waa waa waa." I never had imagined such wailing could come from such a husky frame. It completely took me aback. Now what was I to do? What ever had I done that started him bawling like this? Should I commiserate with him? About what? And why? I was at such a loss, all I could do was leave the room. I called to the new janitor to bring him some water, with instructions to send him down to me as soon as he'd regained his composure. But, after that, I never heard another word from him. Nothing. Neither that day nor any other. He continued to come to school once a week and would spend fifteen minutes swapping stories with the janitors in the courtyard or up on the porch. But then he would leave. On that particular day, a few minutes later, I saw him through my window, leaving by the main gate with his tail between his legs. Then the new janitor came in. Yep, they had demanded five *tomans* from his son before they'd agreed to put his boy's name on the free clothes list for the Town Council. Obviously the janitor was still trying to do in the *nāzem*. I dismissed him and summoned the *nāzem*. The well-digger had clearly wanted to hit the *nāzem*, plain and simple with no introductions. Then the *nāzem* had yelled for the other teachers and the children to come to his aid. Out of fear, the poor fellow had then leapt up onto the wall.

One snowy day in mid-February I met yet another of the parents. The janitor and the *nāzem* clumped upstairs one after the other to bring me the news. They'd obviously smelled something in the wind. This fellow was a tiny man, ostentatiously westernized, carefully groomed and smelling of aftershave lotion. He hadn't even sat down before he was describing his own educational background and his many trips abroad. With all the gleaming hardware on his wrists and fingers, he could have opened a goldsmith shop. He was so tiny, his overcoat was shorter than my suitcoat. At this time of year, in the middle of the term, he wanted to transfer his son from another school over to ours. The son was one of those yellow skinned, lifeless kids you have to beg and cajole before cramming their morning milk and jam down their throats. The boy was in the second grade and had two failures to make up from the first term, both in the same three and a half lessons which our second graders were now studying. The father claimed they had a gardener who had a home in the orchard on their summer place near school. The gardener's boy was one of our students and, according to all reports, an avid studier.

"Obviously, under the protective shadow of Mr. Principal, the children were making excellent progress. In relation to other schools, there was just no comparison..." After more of this flattery, he explained that, for the sake of their child, in the midst of all this snow and cold, they had moved to their summer place. 'The honorable local citizenry have grown enlightened,' thought I. I assured him there was no need for such excessive praise. Indeed, our school which dealt mainly with children of gardeners and water distributers was only too proud to have the son of...I sensed I had annoyed him. I got up, called the *nāzem*, stuck his and his boy's hands into the hand of the *nāzem*, and bid them good day. A half an hour later the *nāzem* returned. He informed me that this fellow had rented out his city house as a high school for three thousand two hundred *tomans* per month. He also had a special request. It so happened he needed a tutor for his son and he was not at all adverse to the principal himself assuming this "inconvenience"...and more of these fat farts...Bits of this information I got from our new janitor. The *nāzem*, I could sense, was fairly watering at the mouth. I told him the fellow obviously wanted assurance that his son would pass and that it would be much better if the *nāzem* himself undertook this charge, provided of course he was careful not to alienate the other teachers and that he avoid a life or death situation to grub up a ten average at the end of the term. That afternoon the *nāzem* arranged to teach one hour every afternoon for one hundred fifty *tomans* a month. Now it was certain that the school would never be closed down for a single afternoon.

From then on, the *nāzem* had the world on a string. He was getting a monthly bonus exactly equal to his salary and all from only one customer. His eyes shone so each morning that I imagined I could see reflections of all the luxuries and modern conveniences in that fellow's home shining in them. His mother was feeling better too, and she had been released from the hospital. The *nāzem* had begun to think about marriage and claimed that his mother, even before she was out of the hospital, had begun searching for a girl. He really had his mind set

n his work, each day a different scheme. One day
e inquired why we didn't have a "Home and School
ociety." He had sat down, done some figuring, and
ome up with fifty to sixty parents who were making
ore than enough to make ends meet. And he claimed
e already had some explicit promises from the
ellow whose son he was teaching. I warned him to
eware of office gossip, to avoid arousing his
olleagues' jealousy, and to then go ahead and do
hatever he pleased. He gave me some paper for the
nvitations. I wrote them out with great grandi-
oquence, even including titles. He carried my draft
o the Office of Education to be mimeographed and,
ater on, passed them out to the children to carry
ack to their daddies. The meeting became official
hen a congregation of twenty parents showed up.
e'd invited seventy and was quite put out that "our
ation" was so stupid and devoid of thought that
nly these few had accepted. I explained that the
nvitation probably smelled fishy to most of them.
hey probably sensed an attempt at extortion.
But it all came off fabulously.
The policeman from the local station stood by the
oor clicking his heels and snapping salutes for
veryone who entered. The teachers sat in a line
rom corner to corner of the auditorium, talking
elf-importantly. The assembly indeed took on an
mposing dignity. The *nāzem* had prepared tea and
ookies and rented a lantern beforehand. Even the
ain had stopped. The auditorium, for the first
ime in its life, was paying dividends. Noise,
ommotion, crowds, hustle and bustle. We made a
olonel in the army the Director and that woman who
opped in on us once a week was voted Deputy. You
an bet this made His Excellency the Colonel all
iles. There was also an old lady who, at the urging
 the Colonel, accepted the position of Treasurer.
ey made the *nāzem* Society Secretary and gave two
 three other titles to the substitute officers.
 was wild. To be only a school principal, seated
 the edge of the abyss, handing out titles--

) 113 (

and with such openhanded generosity. Everyone was happy and smiling. But I kept myself securely on the sidelines. The principalship was position enough for me. The fellow whose son the *nāzem* tutored hadn't come. Instead, he sent a sealed envelope addressed to the principal. We opened it on the spot. First, apologies for being unable to "attain the favour of our presence" tonight, and, second, an "insignificant" contribution inside the envelope. One hundred and fifty *tomans*. The first light had been lit. I spread the money on the Treasurer's desk so it could be duly registered. The Deputy Director, perfumed and toileted, was passing cookies. With each cookie they accepted, the teachers blushed from ear to ear. Meanwhile the janitors busily moved in and out serving tea. In this convivial atmosphere no one gave a thought to the school principal. I felt like a fortune teller reading a crystal ball, content to be sitting on the edge of the abyss. I was deep in these thoughts when I suddenly realized that three or four hundred *tomans* in cash was on the table and eight hundred more had been pledged.

The old lady who was Treasurer hadn't brought her handbag; so those present were obliged to give their approval to temporarily entrust the *nāzem* with the money. "There is no 'me and you' between us. We have complete confidence and trust..." Finally, they wrote up the minutes and affixed their signatures in rows underneath. I signed last of all at the bottom. In a rush of fellow-feeling, the meeting came to a close. I discovered the next day that on that very night, after the meeting concluded, the *nāzem* had gone out and given a banquet for all the teachers.

My first action was to send copies of the minutes to the Office of Education, the Central Personnel Department, the Central Ministerial Office of Public Affairs, and a hundred other places, exactly like a conservative school principal should. Next, I called in that master carpenter and ordered him to put doors on all the toilets within two days time, work which the nāzem was hard pressed to pay for. Then we planted trees along both of the footpaths leading up to school. We changed the volleyball net, purchased a slew of balls, and made a daily schedule of practices in preparation for matchs with other schools. During these giddy days, the physical education inspector suddenly appeared. Everyday he came over to check on how things were progressing. From then on, confusion, crowds and commotion, the likes of which I can't even begin to describe, were the order of the day.

One fine morning when I arrived at school, I was greeted by a ruckus coming from the auditorium. Clang, clunk, crash. It was the sound of pieces of metal coming together, coupled with the panting and wheezing of children. Yes, it was the sound of weights and dumb-bells. The nāzem had gone out and purchased two or three hundred *tomans* worth of exercise equipment and here were our slight, fragile-boned youngsters busily breaking their necks under the load--red faced and pouring sweat. Clank, clunk, crash. What could I say? Should I get angry because he'd gone ahead without getting my authority? As if I had any to delegate. Who was I? As if the money had come out of the school's budget. I'd asked for this myself. First that case with the shoes and clothing, and now this "Home and School Society." As if I had any idea how much he was raking in and handing out? The only money I'd seen was what he'd given to the carpenter. Really, my own mind was completely at ease. They all knew it. The money was that which the parents themselves had donated, and surely they realized how the teachers were spending it. The important thing was that the school's auditorium had a new lease on life and was finally being put to use. At least the children now had a ball to chase after, a set of weights to make them sweat, draw deep breaths to make their chests grow, and help them digest their bread, cheese and stewed lunches. The *nāzem* was content and so were the teachers. There wasn't a single hint of any jealousy and not a word had been raised against them. All that was amiss was that I hadn't enjoined the *nāzem* not to forget the janitors.

15

We gradually began to ready ourselves for the second term examinations. I had kept myself completely out of the first term ones both because I had been new and because I had feared too many cooks might spoil the broth. But, now, I had to take a hand just to see how they made the children sweat. Also, we were obliged to give report cards before the New Year's Holidays. In order to be eligible to enter the New Year, the kids had to have last year's report card, or, at a minimum, grades from two-thirds of the academic year. Thus, one day in late February I summoned all the teachers together for a council meeting and, without further introduction, told them a story about one of my former teaching colleagues who had been so stingy with his grades that every time he had to give out an A+, he was sick for two days afterwards. He taught history in the first cycle of high school, was a young man, and had been to normal school. Yet neither his youth nor his training had had any effect. Every morning when we saw he wasn't feeling well, we knew that the day before he'd been forced to give out an A+. Of course the teachers all laughed. With this encouragement, I felt obliged to tell them another; this one about the mullah who had been my religious law teacher when I was a boy, the one who used to give out grades under his cloak. His hands used to tremble so that his whole cloak shook. It was always a good ten minutes before we could leave. And then, what had we received? He had given the best student a C. It was as if he had given birth to our grades.

) 116 (

That's how dear they were to him. Of course the teachers all laughed again. But this time I didn't feel flattered. I put my jesting aside, and explained to them that it wouldn't be a bad idea if we consulted with one another beforehand about the types of questions on the exam, adding, "I am at your service to help in any way I can..." Then we took a look at the sixth graders with an eye towards determining which of them we might present for the final grade school examination--discussing as well what we could do to make the number of ineligibles smaller. That was the agenda for our meeting.

The following Saturday, examinations began. The dates were the second and third weeks of March. Three of us looked over the exams--myself, the teacher involved, and the nāzem, lest the questions be overly difficult or concern something not covered in the lessons. Then we rang the bell, and proceeded to the auditorium, one behind the other. Ever since we had become the proud owners of weights and dumb-bells, the sign "Athletic Society" hung from the door, and pictures of he-men were more plentiful than ever, papering the wall. Two dilapidated tables were in one corner, along with a pile of handicraft projects, and a bench press stand resembling a crab with its feet fastened to the floor. The handicraft projects consisted of little cardboard cupboards decorated with round flowers made from colored paper, unsanded wooden doll's furniture, inlaid picture frames of three-layer plywood, an Eiffel Tower no bigger than two and a half hand lengths with a top which looked like the minaret on the Shāh Mosque, and a map of Iran with holes drilled in it to represent cities. How many jigsaws had been used up in order to produce this worthless junk? How many cut hands? Just imagine the quarrels at home. And all for what? All to get a better grade in handicrafts. These days were not the days of yore. Nowadays, even Ministers of Education acknowledged that all those names, dates, formulas, and the other lessons learned by heart were not going to help tomorrow's children fill their idle lives in a constructive manner. Nowadays, every child had to learn some kind of skill, craft, trade, or industrial art...so that if nothing should come from all their framed diplomas on the wall, at least their cupboard wouldn't be bare, and they wouldn't die of starvation. What then could be better than a handicrafts program?

Long live cardboard boxes made for shoes and cookies! As if to think that just recently all the children had fathers who could bring surprises home every night, wrapped in their handkerchiefs. And longer live colored oil paper, one page for an *'abbāsi*. And don't forget glue, seventy-five grams for not more than a hundred *dinārs*—or in that vicinity. We import jigsaws by the donkey load, along with safety pins, tile toilets, water piping, enema equipment, and thousands of other pieces of junk. Yet, for every thousand people, you're lucky to find one good enough to open a frame-making shop, or do inlaying work, or exchange his jigsaw for a hacksaw, nuts and bolts, and an adjustable wrench. God bless the father of this educational system, with its handicraft program so successful in increasing the number of sidewalk spice sellers, its grades in deportment, its left face-right face march, and all the borders and lakes of the world; and the exports of Ethiopia to be memorized. And don't forget physical education and handwriting practice. In the old days when we were studying, we only had physical education and handwriting as mortar to fill the cracks between our grades.

How fortunate the children of this generation. They have handicrafts, they have civics, and best of all, they have deportment which is in the hands of the school principals and requires no studying and no midnight oil whatsoever. All you need to know is how to bow and obey. Observe the epigrams on the wall. "Hear no evil, speak no evil," "Learn your

) 118 (

manners from the impolite," and "Peace of mind makes a man content." Really now, isn't all this the embodiment of progress? Progress for the children, for the educational system, and especially for the principals. Why, it's another step towards full authority for the principals. Encounters with things such as this convinced me I had a really important job. Just like a cabinet post. Higher than a cabinet post. I had never realized that one could simply sit down and give out grades to children, and that a grade in deportment counts as much as any other, like grades in important subjects like history, religious law, and arithmetic, and the grade you give is based on criteria like three months ago such and such a kid hid behind the door to your office and gently blew his nose, or whether or not he bowed his head when you were talking with him yesterday. Let the teachers kill themselves trying to make children's minds into sieves so they can pour in their own useless knowledge. Come examination time, they have excess baggage like you around, the principal. Just like a cabinet official, you close the door to your office and, without a second thought, evaluate each child's personality in all its variety with one carelessly given numerical mark pulled from the air. You call this his grade in deportment. Then you give his report card to his parents. They read it with great excitement and delight, show it to all the neighbors, and brag about what a polite child they have. He received twenty in deportment. Wow, what an important job I have. Don't you think so?

All of the written examinations were held in the auditorium. Before each exam, I held a meeting with the children. I explained to them that their fears of the teacher and the examination were completely groundless, that one must have self-confidence, that their teachers had the utmost kindness and...Do you think they heard a word? The moment they entered the door, such a rush they made for the corners of

the auditorium I can't even begin to describe it. To
the places furthermost from view. You would have
thought they were escaping to a refuge. Full of
fear and trembling. One time, they were so bad I
honestly felt they must've gotten a special kind
of pleasure from their own fear and that they
were actually trying to make themselves afraid.
Those who simply walked in, sat down in the front
row, and placed their books on the floor beside
them were incredibly rare. Even if you weren't a
teacher or a principal, you could easily guess
who had made arrangements to sit beside whom. They
helped each other. They sought refuge in each other.
They hid themselves in each other's shadows. They
clung to their books one minute past the deadline.
You don't think that alone--completely alone--
one can confront an examination, do you? A couple
of times, I tried to stand over the shoulder of
one of them to see what he was writing. All of a
sudden, such penmanship...What incredible handwriting. Don't think that it's for nothing that
all the offices need typewriters. I have no idea
what their handwriting teacher had been up to,
although of course it wasn't his fault. You can be
sure their one *toman* pens were not altogether
guiltless. The children stretched their necks to
see over each other's hands with such intensity
that they completely forgot about themselves--
much less about protecting their own paper. And
they hesitated even if they knew an answer. Either
they had suddenly forgotten it, or else they had
a doubt. And what were the examination questions?
"Three cows give so much milk collectively each
day. The first cow gives twice as much as the
second, and the second gives one and half times as
much as the third. Determine how much milk each
cow gives every day." Or, "Children's duties
towards their parents." Or, "Name the rivers of
China." This kind of b.s. These men of tomorrow
were going to be so frightened by these classes

) 120 (

and these examinations and their brains and their
nerves so frayed by terror that by the time they had
their diplomas and their degrees, they really would
be a new breed of men. Men full of fear. Paper bags
full of fear and anxiety. When a person is a
teacher, he doesn't notice such things because the
other side, the party he is dealing with, is hos-
tile. You have to be a principal, meaning you have
to be at the edge of the abyss, eyes fixed everyday, every month, on the arrayal of troops, teachers
on the one hand, students on the other, in order
to understand what that sheet of paper called a
diploma or a degree really means. It certifies that
the owner of this sheet of paper was subject to the
pressure of fear for twelve or fifteen full years,
four to ten times every year, and that his sole
motivating force was fear, fear, and more fear.
   I wasn't able to continue like this for more
than a day. I couldn't identify enough with a
child's mind to be able to comprehend that fear
and that terror, and hence, I wasn't able to feel
any sympathy. Ten years of teaching and giving
out all kinds of low grades had turned my heart
to stone. This was why, despite all my preparation, I dropped the supervision of the examinations
and sought refuge once again in my office...What will
be, will be. In the end, one person wins and another
loses. And, besides, the teachers did have a right.
Don't forget that when they were children and had
gone to school, they had certainly taken their
beatings. Now it was their turn to do the beating.
And this vicious circle wasn't all that small--
nor was it within my grasp--so that I could cut
it off in any one place--in school, or in class,
or in the examinations.
   This is the way it was. Little by little, I was
beginning to realize that I couldn't even be a
school principal.

16 The report cards were ready for the principal's signature two days before New Year's. Two hundred thirty-six signatures takes at least until noon, especially since this was no ordinary signature; it had to be very official and ministry-like. My hand just wasn't used to it. In all the time I was principal, I never once signed the ledger. In all the schools I had ever been in before coming here, I had always avoided signing attendance books. I had observed many of the "government ration-eaters" in other offices as well as my own colleagues practicing their signatures when they had nothing to do, left and right, on anything they could get their hands on. Look at the blotter of every office drudge and witness an exhibition of signatures. Even he realizes that a man's signature reflects his personality. Two or three quick little humps, then a thick fat line pulled from left to right and curlicued underneath, the date fixed below in clear characters. Then a big circle drawn under the thick line in such a way so as not to touch the others. Finally, a diagonal through the center as a final flourish. Completely official. This was all, of course, a kind of practice for the Ministry. Now that I was a principal, I could easily comprehend this. I never used to understand fully how the principal of some school or the lowly clerk of some office even dreamed of making it to the Ministry, let alone actually do so. By six dozen signatures, each one reflecting a personality, then, a half a yard of slippery tongued compliments to entice the snake from the hole. Another way is to kiss everybody's ass and develop a full set of facial mannerisms. There is no single method. There are twelve different methods, like a set of silverware—each one designed to perform a different function. With one you pull the fish from the pot. With another you scale it...As I signed the report cards one after the other, this was

) 122 (

what I thought about. Suddenly my eyes came across
a familiar name--the son of the Colonel we had
elected Director of the Home and School Society.
The boy was in the sixth grade. His clothes were
more chic and neatly pressed than any of the
teachers'. Thanks to the weight given to the in-
signia on his father's shoulders, he was allowed
to be absent two or three times a week and to
show up late everyday. Since his father was Mr.
Everything in the Society, the nāzem obviously
didn't exactly hound the boy. I looked over his
grades. All of them were average, no room for any
objections. And I am going to have to give this
boy a grade in deportment at the end of the year...
There were no grounds. What should I do?...Wow!
I suddenly lost all interest in this case. I just
then realized that from the beginning of the year
until now we had been judging all of the children
solely on the basis of their fathers' financial
situations, just like this Colonel's son who, because of the weight of his father's position, never
studied a lick. I saw now that in all the time I
had been here the students whose fathers weren't
well off seemed to me to be the smarter ones, the
more educable, and the more eager. Those whose
fathers were in the chips were slower learners,
more stupid, more phlegmatic, and more discouraging.
The nāzem, of course, would have nothing to do with
such opinions. He believed in following the letter
of the law, while, at the same time, exacting his
own fair share--just like he did with the Colonel's
son. He closed his eyes to one, was brutally strict
with another, and then, two days later, reversed
himself. In short, his was a policy of fear and
hope; and that in fact was what made the school
run. But me? It seemed as if I had prejudged all
the children. How fortunate that the authority to
give grades wasn't mine, and that that which was
came at the end of the year. I'd heard that there
had been a time in military schools when they had

given out grades according to height. Now I realized
that here at school, if the authority to give grades
had been mine, I would have given them out according to their fathers' financial situations.
  But what was most laughable of all was that with
this type of thinking, I was the one who was trying
to stamp out poverty. It now hit me that this attitude of mine was, in effect, a justification for
poverty, not a condemnation of it. I had considered
that the freedom from want of some was abominable
because it caused the poverty of the water dis-
tributors and the gardeners. And for this reason
I had worked to stamp it out. But within the four
walls of the school was I doing the right thing...
Someone who tries to make reforms and improvements
from a realm of authority no bigger than the tip of
his nose is the most ridiculous man in the world--
and this was my realm of authority, not even as big
as the tip of my nose. Mine went only as far as
my own mind. In a situation others had set up, the
school had become for me a kind of geography
problem. After five or six months, I now realized
my reckonings had not been rational. Rather, they
had been emotional. I had heard rumors that the
nāzem was collecting a few *tomans* from two or three
other places. Now I realized "this was the price
of atonement for my sins." These are indeed the
kinds of things which make the school run. His
practical harshness made up for my emotional weak-
nesses. All things considered, I couldn't do without
him. He was a man of action. He decided on his
work, went out and did it. Every move he made in
everything he did had a specific purpose. He
closed his eyes to all other considerations. This
was why he could function and I couldn't If only
I weren't principal. I wasn't cut out for this.
Ah...freedom...The Colonel's son's report card
had grown sweaty under my hand. I dried it with
great care and precision and signed my name. But
my signature came out so badly and looked so

) 124 (

ridiculous that it reminded me of the janitor's. His Excellency, the Colonel, was surely going to get upset, wondering how in the world an illiterate with such bad penmanship ever made principal. For even a Colonel knows that a signature reflects a man's personality.

17

Towards the end of the spring New Year's holidays, I went to visit my third grade teacher. The nāẓem had never gotten along with him, so I was obliged to make my arrangements with the fifth and sixth grade arithmetic teacher, the one who had shown an interest in all those speeches and carryings on. Through him, I found out where the boy was, which jail, and in what cell block. As we set off, the first bit of news he gave me was that the Chief of Education had been changed. Rumor had it that one of my former classmates had come to take his place.

"Incredible. Why? What was the matter with the old Chief?"

"What can I say? They claim he stepped on the toes of one of the members of Parliament. Didn't you hear about it?"

"How? Where was I to find out?"

"Nothing...They say two of the election heavies for the district representative were getting their salaries paid by the Office of Education. New Year's Eve, the Chief cut off their salaries."

"Incredible! Then he was trying to make reforms too. Poor devil."

Our discussion turned to how, "praise be to God," our school was quiet, peaceful, and completely in order, and how all the teachers cooperated with each other. Through it all, he made it quite clear that lately the nāẓem had grown a little too big for his britches. 'The nāẓem must have come up with some

more private customers,' I thought, and hence raised rumblings among his fellow teachers. I changed the subject to the life of the third grade teacher.
He was scheduled to have his salary terminated as of the twenty-first of March. His university classes had been stopped for some time now. Obviously, his mother and father sent him nothing. They had nothing to do with him anymore. They'd severed relations long ago. There was no organization to help him out. So, for the time being, all he had was the daily bread the jail provided. Luckily he didn't smoke and...This was the course of our conversation.

A swarm of people crowded around the jail door. Everybody and his brother from all walks of life. Old villagers in their felt hats, local dandies in the latest Paris fashions, village women in their bright, flower-print dresses, aunts and sisters with their bundles and their babies, even two or three mullahs and green turbaned *sayyeds*. We registered, duly recording the names of our father, mother, I.D. card number, and where it was issued. Then, we awaited our turn. Instead of our feet being tired, it was our hands that ached and drifted off to sleep until our turn came. From this room to that room, this hallway to that, in each one an inspection and a search for something different. Finally, an iron-barred cell with the third grade teacher inside... Wow! How healthy he looked. He looked like a real somebody. Involuntarily, I thought of the fourth grade teacher who was still confined to a plaster cast. We both expressed our happiness at seeing each other again. We exchanged greetings. The guard came over, took the packages we'd brought, thanked us, and left. What else was there to say? Should I ask him why he got himself into this mess? He obviously was enjoying himself more here than he had at school in front of a class. The color of one of his hands had changed. It was obvious that under his coat his arm was bandaged from the wrist up. But he was healthy and in good spirits. There is such a thing called faith, and he had plenty of it. He considered himself lucky, had no gripes whatsoever, and claimed that jail at least had been kind of a lesson for him. Finally, I asked:

"Have they given you a record yet, or are they still making a decision?"

"They tested me, Mr. Principal, and it didn't turn out too badly."

"What do you mean?"

"I mean I didn't get off scot free, but my name is still on the jail's ration list, so my mind's at ease. The worst is over now."

What else should I say? I had nothing more. I said goodbye, left him alone with the arithmetic teacher, and went outside. I walked back and forth in front of the jail gate, until visiting hours ended, thinking all the while about the kind of jail I had constructed for myself. I mean the one that filthy rich philanthropist had built, where I, under my own volition and free will, had voluntarily imprisoned myself. They had brought this fellow here by force. He had a right to his peace of mind. But I had gone of my own volition. What could I do? What about the nāẕem? Hey, if the new Chief of Education is one of my former classmates, why not go to him and ask him to put the nāẕem in my place? Or, maybe the arithmetic teacher?...The arithmetic teacher came outside and we headed off. I didn't have anything more to talk with him about so when we got to the corner, I said goodbye, grabbed a cab, and went straight to the Office of Education.

Although this was the tenth day of the New Year, the traditional exchange of visits was still going on. Come over to our house, go over to their house, cookies and tea from all sides. A new year and a new Chief. A conjunction of two lucky stars. I entered, blurted a hello, congratulations on the New Year, and the rest of the usual courtesies. Yes, it was him alright. One of our class dunderheads. At the end of our third year, I had tried to help him memorize two couplets from the famous *Lāmiyat ul-'Arab* poem. But he couldn't even understand what every street corner beggar who chanted from the Koran could. And now that he was Chief, he still couldn't. Obviously, the conjunction of lucky stars hadn't understood me very well, because here he was, at the top of the heap, and I was still Mr. Principal.

   The desk was still clean and shiny, like a reception room for new brides. But the ashtray was now filled with ashes and cigarette butts. He had a cigarette in his hand himself. He got up to greet me. Smack, smooch. We exchanged kisses on the cheek. He cleared a spot for me to sit right beside him. Office of Education "ration-eaters" lined the room from corner to corner. "Sincerest congratulations ..." "I have heard so many wonderful things about him..." "The honor of your presence..." Vilification of the former chief, more excessive compliments, and b.s. Two men built like they belonged in the pit of a House of Strength or else beside the ballot box on election day, served cookies. "You don't suppose these two are the same ones who canned the Chief of Education, do you?..." I was about to throw my cookies back on the platter when I realized how stupid that would be. I finished my cigarette and put my lips close to the new Chief's ear. In a whisper, I inquired about the former Chief, and those two men. He didn't say a word. He only gave me a beseeching look. Then, I seized the opportunity to clarify the third grade teacher's plight, and asked him to do what he could to keep them from standing in the way of the boy's salary. It wasn't until I was outside that I remembered I had gone to visit the Chief on altogether different business.

18 Yesterday, once again, another mess occurred. At least the first month of Spring was over so we could all relax again. It was now the fourth week in April, and the rolling drum beats of disgrace had arisen. The school day was nearly over, when a father and mother entered my office with a child between them. One was steaming mad, the other pale and shaken. The child looked like a kewpie doll. Greetings. They sat down. Dear God, what is it now that's happened? I had reached the absolute end of the line. I kept telling myself I should drop everything and quit; but my apathy wouldn't let me. I lacked the energy. What's happened that brings you and your wife here to honor us today? The man signalled to his wife. She got up, took the child by the hand, and went outside. The father and I remained behind--he reeking indignation and and disgust, me full of questions. He didn't say a word. He was allowing himself time for his anger to come to a full boil. I was caught in a trap. I took out a cigarette and offered him one. He refused it, waving it away like a bothersome fly in front of his nose. I lit up with the thought that this fellow must really have a problem to have gotten so up tight that he had to bring his whole family along. There must be a danger in the air that's made him mobilize all his forces like this.

"Well," I inquired, "What can I do for you?"

Suddenly he burst out: "If I were the principal of this school and this thing happened, I'd cut out my own guts. You should be embarrassed, man! Go hand in your resignation before the people of this neighborhood rip you apart bit by bit, cut off your ears and run away with them. Our children come here to study and learn good morals. They don't come to ..."

"What is this nonsense, Āqā? What is Your Excellency trying to say?"

I made a move as if I were about to throw him out. But really, you know I couldn't do that without first

finding out what was bothering him so. Imagine. The
s.o.b., cussing me out in my own room, while I, "in
the line of duty,"...and in this way to boot, to
the principal of a grade school. He seemed to have
forgotten that at the bare minimum the fate of one
year of his son's life was in my hands. People
like this get crushed under automobiles everyday and
no one is there to ask why did this happen, or who
is to blame. This small fry probably has a legitimate
gripe. But what's it to me?

"My reputation is ruined. The reputation of
one hundred years of my family is ruined. If
I don't close down the doors of your school,
I'm not my father's son. What am I to do with
this boy now, huh? Chastity is endangered
in this school. The police station has heard
about it. The medical examiner knows about
it. There's a record five pages long. Now
you're asking me what I'm trying to say? I'm
saying this job and this title are more than
you can handle. I'm saying that I'm going to
see to it you go to court and that they throw
you out on your ear..."

He was yelling and I was yelling back--like a
pair of rabid dogs at each others' throats. The door
opened and the nāẓem entered--in the nick of time
to save me. If he'd come in a minute later, God only
knows what might have happened. At the same time
that the boy's father and I were cussing each other
out, the mother, with the boy in tow, had been
putting the case more succinctly and plainly to
the nāẓem, who ordered the seducer dragged from his
classroom...The nāẓem suggested we ring the bell
and chastise the villain on the spot in front of all
the children. And so we did, which is to say that
this time I myself leaped into the ring. He was
a burly lad, one of the fifth graders, neatly
dressed, pink cheeked, with a lachymiosis scar on

) 130 (

one side of his face. He himself would have made a
much better target for seduction than that little
kewpie doll. The boy was obviously from a well-to-do
family because he didn't expect anyone to address
him with the diminutive second person singular.
We dragged him in front of all the children, beat
him and kicked him about. The new janitor brought
some freshly cut switches from the neighbor's
orchard; and I broke three of them over the boy's
head and shoulders. I was so savage that if the
switches hadn't broken, I might have killed him.
The *nāzem* had to come to the rescue. After he in-
tervened, they carried what was left of the boy into
the office and dismissed the children. I went back
to my room and, in a bitter, wounded state, collapsed
into my chair. There was no news from the father,
the mother, or their kewpie doll. 'What I should
have done,' I thought to myself, 'was to have given
him the beating.' I was wet with sweat and my
mouth had a bitter taste to it. All the insults I
should have shouted back at that man and hadn't had
formed a sediment in the bottom of my mouth. It
had grown acrid and galling, like a snake's tail.
Why did you put yourself in this predicament, huh?
A mad dog has set upon the children. For God's sake,
why had I beat him? Why hadn't I let the *nāzem*, who
is so much more experienced and cold-blooded, take
over? What is preserving the children's chastity
to me? Do you think they made me school principal
so I could watch over the lower half of their
bodies? A school in the middle of nowhere or, for
that matter, anywhere, in the spring season, when a
kid's piss has started to foam, if you're the
principal or some other donkey is--what difference
does it make? This kid probably can't even play
with his female cousins. All the girls in his family
probably have to cover themselves from the time they
reach ten or twelve years old. "Idiot, you think
you've cured a large ache with a beating. Why oh
why did you beat him? What's it to you? And the way

you beat him. They say you killed him...You don't think he's been permanently hurt?..." I suddenly got a notion to go see what horrible misfortune I had wrought. I got to my feet and called one of the janitors. It was obvious that they had spread the word. He brought me some water, poured it into my hands, and I washed my face, trying all the while not to let him see the quivering in my hands. He bent down and whispered in my ear that the boy was the son of the Director of the Bus Company, that he'd taken a really bad beating, and that they had done all they could to clean him up before letting him go, wiping away the blood from I don't know where before sending him home. These kinds of obsequious services...Idiot. Here he is trying to help me unburden my heart. He doesn't even realize that I had first made up my mind and then turned into a mad dog. It was then that I realized I had beaten someone who really had deserved it. With the blows of my fists and feet over every single part of his body, I had uprooted, torn out, and cast aside all the effects of his pampered upbringing and twenty-four-hour-a-day gluttony. This was certainly the first time in his life he ever had such a rub down. 'Stupid little savage. Your piss has started making foam. Why don't you go jerk off like everyone else, instead of messing around with little boys and causing them to end up like this in a police station and a medical examiner's office? And all this in a school in which I am the principal.'

Surely things like this happen in other places. But you can bet they don't wash their dirty linen in public like this stupid mother and father, who have gone everywhere broadcasting their own rape and hence increasing its stink. Is a man supposed to pick up the lower half of his child's body, or, in this man's words, his family's chastity, and put it on the street corner so the local police department and doctor can examine it to verify what happened, to get a record written up? Why and for whom? Just to throw the school's principal out of work? To do this you don't need a chastity record. One hammer and sickle underneath these pictures of the Achaemenid tombs was plenty. Curses on all their stupid heads. With fathers and mothers like this, children have a right to turn out to be pederasts, pretty boys, thieves, and liars. These schools ought to be first opened up to the parents. How I wished I'd applied my fists and feet to that father with the impudent mouth...With these thoughts swimming in my head, I arrived home.

My wife opened the door, and her eyes opened wide. Whenever she is afraid, her eyes do this. I explained it all quickly so she wouldn't think I'd killed someone. She was stunned. I mean she didn't say a word. Cold water, the strongest vodka I could find, cigarette after cigarette. It was no use. A bone had caught in my throat and it wouldn't go down. My hands continued to shake. Lighting up my fourth cigarette, I commenced:

> "Do you know, woman? That boy's daddy is loaded. He is going to drag this thing all the way to the Public Prosecutor's Office and worse. There is going to be a real stink before this is finished. The principalship--you can forget it. But I really hope it goes all the way to court. For one whole year I've given myself ulcers. Now I'm sick of it. I hope somebody asks me, 'Why did you beat one of the children like that; why did you use physical punishment?' Damn it, a school principal has a lot of things to say which must be said someday..."

She got up, went to the telephone, and got a hold of two or three of my friends in the Public Prosecutor's Office. I explained the situation to them over the phone so they could be on the alert.

The next day, the seducer didn't come to school. The *nāẓem* told me how the incident had occurred. The

two of them had gone to the seducer's home under the
pretext of looking at his stamp collection. That
was where it had happened. Screams and cries for
help, interference by the parents of both, warnings
and threats, and overnight in the police station.
And now everybody in the neighborhood knew about it.
The nāzem said that he too thought it would wind
up in the Public Prosecutor's Office. I spent the
whole week awaiting my summons. I went to school
every morning and every afternoon and, like Nebuchad-
nezzar, simply stood by the window gazing out.

In all this time, there was no sign of the seducer,
nor the seduced, nor of the chastity-worshipping
parents, nor the Director of the Bus Company. It was
all as if nothing had happened. The children came
and they went; they still raced to be first for
drinking water, they still fell down every minute on
the minute, and instead of games they still fought.
The teachers continued to delay two or three minutes
before going to class, and they still left home late
for school. The nāzem, with that same clump, clump,
still marched around like Bismarck, managing the
school's affairs. Only I remained, alone, with a
whole world of anticipation and unsaid words.
Until, finally, it arrived...A summons with a
specific time, set for the day after tomorrow, in
such and such a district office, before such and
such an examining magistrate from the Public Prosecutor's Office. At long last, I was going to have my
day in court. Somebody was finally going to listen
to me.

19

Until the day of the summons two days
later, I didn't so much as budge from the house.
Instead, I sat down and wrote out on paper a summary
of everything I had to say--stuff which, despite all
its nonsense, was enough to keep any Minister of
Education busy on an eight year program. At exactly

the fixed time, I went to the Public Prosecutor's Office. A specific room and a special magistrate. I opened the door. Hello. But before I could introduce myself and take out my summons, he anticipated me. He brought over a chair, placed it beside me, ordered tea and began:

"Now, now, there is no need for all this. This was nothing but a trifle. It's solved now. We didn't want to cause you any trouble..."

A cold sweat broke out over my body.

After I finished my tea, I took that same paper with the seal of the Public Prosecutor's Office on it and wrote out my letter of resignation. I addressed it to that stupid former classmate of mine, the new Chief of Education, and dropped it in the mail.

GLOSSARY

ābādi.

The word ābād can mean "built [up]" or "flourishing" and is often used in place names as the second member of a compound; e.g., Khorramābād.
Ābādi means an "inhabited, cultivated, or flourishing place," i.e., a village.

Abāzar.

One of the first followers of the Prophet Moḥammad, Abāzar or Abuzar is known as a very religous and humble early Moslem. For information about another Companion of the Prophet, see *Salmān*.

'abbāsi.

Dating, as its name indicates, from the reign of Shah 'Abbās the Great (1571-1629), *'abbāsi* is the name of a coin which was the equivalent of two hundred *dinārs* or four *shāhis* during the early 20th century. For more, see *dinār* and *shāhi*.

'Ali.

The cousin and son-in-law of the Prophet Moḥammad and the father of Ḥasan and Ḥosayn, 'Ali (d. 660 A.D.)

was the fourth caliph of Islam. More importantly for Iranian Shi'ite Moslems, 'Ali is considered the first of twelve *emāms*, including his two sons, who are held to have been the legitimate successors to Mohammad. For more, see *emām* and H.A.R. Gibb's article "'Alī b. Abī Ṭālib" in *Encyclopaedia of Islam: New Edition* 1: 381-386.

Āqā.

An honorific used to address and refer to males, *āqā* is not, however, used as "Mr." can be in English to refer to oneself. *Āqā* can appear before a proper name (either a surname alone or with a first name) as in the phrase *Āqā-ye Tehrāni* ("Mr. Tehrani") or after a first name as in the phrase *Ahmad Āqā*. The second construction can be used in addressing members of the servant class, intimate friends, and relatives. *Āqā* by itself can mean "Mister" or "Sir" as in *bebakhshid, āqā*, which means "Excuse me, sir."

Bābā Ṭāher.

An eleventh century Iranian poet and Ṣufi (Moslem mystic) from Hamadān about whose life little is known, Bābā Ṭāhir is credited with the composition of a group of famous quatrains expressive of Ṣufi themes. The quatrains are translated by A.J. Arberry in *Poems of a Persian Ṣufi* (Cambridge: Heffer, 1937). The handiest scholarly introduction to Bābā Ṭāher is V. Minorsky's article "Bābā-Ṭāhir" in *Encyclopaedia of Islam: New Edition* 1: 800-842.

Besmellāh.

Besmellāh is an abbreviated form of the phrase *besmellāhe r-rahmāne r-rahim*, which translates as "In the name of God the Merciful, the Compassionate." This Arabic phrase, with which the Koran begins and which prefaces nearly all of the chapters of the Koran, is a popular expression of piety today for Iranian Moslems in many contexts.

blacksmith in Balkh.

Perhaps originating with Ferdowsi, "the blacksmith in Balkh" has become a proverbial image of a person who is to be blamed for some misdeed when the person really responsible is not known.

chādor.

A veil-like, full length covering worn by many Moslem women in Iran, the *chādor* represents, for some, compliance to Islamic regulation that women cover themselves when in public.

dinār.

An originally gold coin in use in various periods of the Islamic Near East, the *dinār* in Iran in recent times is an unrelated coin of little value equivalent to 1/100 of a *rial*. For more, see *rial*.

Emām.

The word *emām* can generally signify a Moslem religious leader, such as the *emām-e jom'eh* or the person who leads the Friday community prayer. It also specifically refers in Iran to any one of the twelve early Shi'ite leaders, beginning with 'Ali and ending with the so-called Hidden Emām, who are revered as the legitimate successors to the Prophet Mohammad by the Twelver Shi'ite sect of Islam. For more, see 'Ali.

Emāmzādeh.

The word *emāmzādeh* literally means "born of [an] emām" and signifies either a descendant of a Shi'ite *emām* or a shrine, of which there are a great number in Iran, built in the honor of such a person. For more, see *emām*.

The Four Discourses.

Called *Chahār Māqaleh* in Persian, Nezāmi 'Aruzi's *The Four Discourses* is a most important 12th century prose work describing four classes of court figures: secretaries, poets, astrologers, and physicians. It has been translated by E. G. Browne in *Revised Translation of the Chahār Maqāla* (London: Cambridge University, 1921).

hayn.

The twenty-second letter of the Persian alphabet, *hayn* represents the same uvular plosive sound as does the letter *qāf* [A.K.S. Lambton, *Persian Grammar* (Cambridge: University Press, 1960), p. xviii].

iveh.

The name of a very inexpensive slip-on footwear, *ivehs* are made of coarse, canvas-like material with leather or more often cloth soles or with discarded pieces of tire rubber.

ājjī.

Hājjī is the title given to a Moslem male who has made the *hajj* or holy pilgrimage to Mecca which is incumbent at least once in a lifetime upon Moslems with the means to do so.

ājji Firuz.

Hājji Firuz (more often pronounced Hāji Firuz) is the name given to the minstrel figure who appears in blackface and red garb throughout the spring New Year's holidays singing and dancing and often accompanied by one or two other such individuals. A symbol of the joy of the new year, people who gather around to watch and listen to the Hājji Firuz often give him something for his efforts.

asan.

Son of 'Ali and older brother of Hosayn, Hasan is the second *emām* for the Twelver Shi'ite sect of Islam. Hasan gave up his claim to the caliphate of Islam after

) 139 (

the murder of his father 'Ali, presumably because of an aversion to politics and war. For more, see Ḥosayn.

Ḥosayn.

Hasan's younger brother, Ḥosayn is revered by Twelver Shi'ite Moslems as the third emām, and as the tragic hero of the unsuccessful revolt against the forces of Yazid, the Caliph, at Karbalā in A.D. 680. For a detailed summary of Ḥosayn's life, there is L. Veccia Vaglieri's article "Husayn b. 'Alī," *Encyclopaedia of Islam: New Edition* 3: 607-615.

Kalileh and Demneh.

An originally Indian collection of animal fables sometimes known as the Bidpai tales, *Kalileh and Demneh* (the names of the two principal characters) reached Iran through both Pahlavi and Arabic redactions of the tales. One English translation of some of the tales is S.A.N. Wollaston's *Tales Within Tales* (New York: Dutton, 1909).

khān.

A word of Turkish origin, *khān* was formerly used as a title for kings and princes and then for aristocrats and other important persons. In recent times, the word *khān* has lost special significance and is often used as an honorific with reference to any male to whom respect is intended.

Khuli.

A figure cited proverbially for cruelty, Khuli is popularly held responsible by many Iranian Shi'ite Moslems for the beheading of Ḥosayn, the third emām. According to L. Veccia Vaglieri, *Encyclopaedia of Islam: New Edition* 3: 611, this individual was called Khawalī and was, on account of fear, unable to perform the beheading which was carried out by Sinōn.

...cheh.

Kucheh can mean a "small area or neighborhood in a ...ty" (kuy = neighborhood in a city + *cheh* = diminu-...ve suffix) or a "street," but it more commonly re-...rs to generally narrow lanes or alleys.

...miyat ul-'Arab.

This famous pre-Islamic Arabic poem is translated ... M. C. Hillmann in "Shanfarā's *Lāmiyat al-'Arab:* ... Translation," *Literature East and West* 15 (1971): 1-138.

Mirror for Princes.

This famous 11th century Persian prose work written ... Kaykāvus ibn Iskandar ibn Qābus, a ruler of the ...spian region of Iran, and addressed to his son is ...aracterized by Reuben Levy as a combination of "the ...nctions of popular educator, manual of political ...nduct and text book of ethics, with expediency as ...s motto" (p. ix) in Levy's translation, *A Mirror for ...inces* (Dutton: New York, 1951).

...nkar.

Monkar and Nakir are the names of the two angels who, ...cording to Moslem tradition, examine the dead after ...eir burial. Those who prove themselves among the ...ithful in this examination are then left alone until ...surrection Day; but those who are sinners are subject ... punishment by the two angels.

...slim ibn 'Aqīl.

A cousin of Emām Hosayn, Muslim ibn 'Aqīl was sent ...om Mecca to Kūfa by Hosayn to determine the strength ... the supporters of the cause of 'Ali and the Shi'ites. ...slim, who later urged Hosayn to come to Kūfa to lead the movement, was martyred by supporters of the Caliph Yazid. For more, see *'Ali, Ḥasan,* and *Ḥosayn.*

Nakir.

See *Monkar.*

nāẓem.

The word *nāẓem* basically means "arranger," "organizer" or "one who keeps order." In the context of an institution such as a school, the *nāẓem* is the person who, und the supervision of the principal or director, is respon ible for the daily operations of the school.

qāf.

Qāf is the twenty-fourth letter of the Persian alphabet. For more, see *ghayn.*

qanāt.

A *qanāt* is a "gently sloping tunnel dug horizontally into an alluvial fan until the water table is pierced. Water filters into the tunnel, runs down its gradual slope, and emerges on the surface as a stream" [P. W. English, *City and Village in Iran* (Madison: University of Wisconsin, 1966), p. 30]. For a diagram of a typical *qanāt,* see English, *City and Village,* p. 31.

rial.

The basic unit of currency in Iran today (actually written and pronounced *riyāl*), one hundred *dināzs* equal one *rial,* and ten *rials* equal one *toman.* One *rial* is equivalent to $.014.

Rostam.

The greatest hero in Iranian mythology and the most

important character in Ferdowsi's epic *Shāhnāmeh*, Rostam appears in English literature as one of the two protagonists in Matthew Arnold's famous "Sohrab and Rustum." The handiest translation of Ferdowsi's *Shāhnāmeh* is Reuben Levy's *The Epic of Kings* (Chicago: University of Chicago, 1967).

Sa'di.

The author of a *divān* (collected shorter poems), the *Golestan*, and the *Bustān*, Sa'di (13th century) is one of the four or five most important medieval Persian poets. His most popular work is translated by Edward Rehatsek in *The Gulistan or Rose Garden of Sa'di* (London: Allen & Unwin, 1964).

Salmān.

"Salmān represents the first contact between Iran and Islam...A Persian who journeyed from his homeland in search of the true Prophet, Salmān came to Arabia where he became one of the closest companions of the Prophet of Islam to the extent that the Prophet called him one of his family. Salmān was also a close companion of 'Ali and is one of the great saints in Shi'ism. He plays a major role in the religious consciousness of all Shi'ites, especially the Persians. In him they find their close connexion with the family of the Prophet, whom they particularly love and revere" [S. H. Nasr, *Iran (Persia)* (Tehran: Offset Press, 1973), p. 112-113].

sangak.

The word *sangak* literally means "small stone" (*sang* = stone + -*ak* = diminutive suffix) and usually signifies a popular unleavened bread baked on small pebbles in a special oven.

sayyed.

The word can mean "sir" or "leader" or refer to Moḥammad the Prophet, but is generally used as a title to refer to any descendant of the Prophet (i.e., through his daughter Fāṭemeh).

Shāh 'Abd al-'Aẓim.

'Abd al-'Aẓim was a descendant of 'Ali. His shrine in Rayy, south of Tehran, is today an important pilgrimage and worship site for Shi'ite Moslems, For more, see *'Ali* and *emāmzādeh*.

shāhi.

Literally meanings "pertaining to the Shāh," *shāhi* is the name of a coin in use in the early 20th century equivalent to fifty *dinārs*. For more, see *dinār*.

toman.

A basic unit of currency in Iran today, the *toman* (literary pronunciation and spelling is *tumān*) consists of ten *rials* and is the equivalent of $.14.

yā 'Ali.

An exclamatory phrase meaning "O 'Ali," *yā 'Ali* is a pious invocation of the name of the *emām*, used, for example, when some difficult physical chore is undertaken.